汉
Chinese-

Shower of Flowers:

彩色的花雨（上）

Tales from Beijing Opera (I)

Better Link Press

目

录

CONTENTS

致读者

要学好一种语言，必须多听、多说、多读、多写。要学好汉语也不例外，必须多听普通话，多阅读汉语作品。

《文化中国·汉英对照阅读丛书》是一套开放的系列，收入其中的主要为当代中国作家的散文、故事、小说等。我们编辑这套汉英对照读物的目的是帮助你阅读欣赏原汁原味的当代中国文学或非文学作品，让你在学习现代汉语、提高汉语阅读水平的同时，了解中国社会、中国文化、中国历史，以及当代中国人民的生活。我们采用汉英对照的办法，是为了帮助你更好地欣赏这些作品，对照英语译文你可以知道自己是不是真正正确地理解了这些汉语原作的意思。

希望你能喜欢。

—— 编者

To the Reader

Acquisition of proficiency in a foreign language calls for diligent practices in listening, speaking, reading, and writing. Learning Chinese is no exception. To a student of Chinese, extensive reading exercises are as important as constant exposure to spoken Mandarin.

Cultural China: Chinese-English Readers series is an open-ended series of collections of writings in Chinese, mostly essays and short stories by contemporary Chinese writers. Our purpose in putting together this bilingual series is to help you enjoy contemporary Chinese literature and other writings in their authentic, unadulterated flavor and to understand the Chinese society, culture, history, and the contemporary life of the Chinese people as you learn the language and hone your reading skills. A bilingual text will assist you in better savoring these works and in checking your understanding of the Chinese original against the English translation.

We hope you will like this volume.

– the Editor

关于《彩色的花雨》和黄裳

作者第一次进戏院的时候还是个孩子。他常常是站在舞台边瞪大双眼看着演出。之后他经历过很多的变动，但是第一印象难以抹去，收入本书的京剧故事片段在很大程度上保留了无法抹去的最初印象。因此，第一次捧读这一伟大的、充满异域情调的现实艺术的朋友们会发现这些故事坦诚真挚又不傲慢。

黄裳（1919—）：原名容鼎昌。1940年开始散文创作，后从事新闻记者工作。撰有大量散文、杂文、剧评、游记、读书随笔，迄今出版专著四十余种，其中包括《锦帆集》、《锦帆集外》、《关于美国兵》、《旧戏新谈》、《山川历史人物》、《榆下说书》、《银鱼集》等。他还翻译了屠格涅夫的《猎人日记》、冈察洛夫的《一个平凡的故事》、萨尔蒂科夫—谢德林的《歌略夫里奥夫家族》等。

About the Book

The author was only a child when he first entered a Chinese theater. Very often he merely stood beside the stage and stared with wide-open eyes at what was going on. Since then he has been through many changes, however, first impressions are not easy to erase. These fragments of opera stories that he has collected in this volume have preserved to a great extent those indelible earliest impressions. Because of this, friends who come into contact with this great, exotic and realistic art for the first time may find these writings candid and sincere but not presumptuous.

HUANG Shang (1919-), whose real name is RONG Dingchang, started prose writing in 1940 and worked later as a journalist. His prolific writings range over prose articles, theatrical reviews, travel reportage and commentaries on books he read. His more than forty published works include *Boat with Brocade Sails*, *Beyond the Boat with Brocade Sails*, *On American G.I.s*, *New Discussions on Old Drama*, *Sketches of a Sportsman*, *Mountains and Rivers*, *History*, *Personalities*, *Talking About Books Under the Shade of an Elm*, *Silver Fish*, etc. He has also translated into Chinese *Sketches of a Sportsman* by I.S. Turgenev, *A Common Story* by Goncharov, *The Golovlyov Family* by Saltykov Shchedrin.

序

　　中国的舞台艺术有着悠久的历史和广阔的活动天地。迄今遍布全国城乡，远及域外，还有上百种不同的地方剧种在活动。其中传统最久远、最成熟、影响也最大的是京剧。

　　京剧的形成、壮大，是吸收了多种地方剧种的滋养，经过戏剧工作者和观众长久的改进、磨合、丰富、提高而形成今天的面貌的。京剧是一种歌舞并重、有独特表演风格的歌舞剧。与西方舞台剧不同的是，它的显著特色可以用这样简要的语言加以表述：凡表达角色的内心活动或人物意愿时，无不采取广义的歌唱的方式，即使对白也不例外；凡是形体动作，无论规模大小，形式繁简，无不以舞蹈手段表现。

　　很久以来，中国戏剧的传统形式多是以长篇、完整的故事出现的，其中不可避免会有穿插、松懈的场次，也必然会有精炼精彩的段落。从观众欣赏角度出发，这些突出而出色的场次，就被破格重视而保留了下来，成为经常演出的"折子戏"。

Preface

China's stage art goes back a long way and commands a broad stage that encompasses the country's cities, towns and villages. Its appeal is felt beyond its borders. Close to a hundred varieties of opera with distinct regional flavors and origins thrive to this day. The genre that boasts the longest tradition, highest degree of maturity and widest impact is Beijing opera.

In its formation and development, Beijing opera has benefited from the nourishment of various regional forms of opera. It has been both refined and enriched and has become what it is today due to the interaction of and mutual accommodation made by people in the trade, and by audiences. Beijing opera is a form of theatrical performance that gives equal weight to singing and choreographed acting, from which it derives its unique style. To put it simply, quite unlike Western stage performances, Beijing opera distinguishes itself by its ubiquitous use of song and dance in the broad sense to express the inner feelings and aspirations of its characters, even in its dialogue. All physical movements, large or small, simple or intricate, are, without exception, executed as dance.

For a long time Chinese opera had a tradition of enacting complete sagas, with inevitable, somewhat irrelevant interludes as well as brilliant scenes and acts. These extraordinary scenes and acts have been preserved, in an exceptional concession to popular demand, as "zhe zi xi" or, operatic highlights that figure in often performed repertoires.

由于民族艺术具有通性，京剧的表演特色与中国画种的"大写意"也往往有暗合、相通的地方。简洁处便简到极处。京剧场上几个小卒可以代表千军万马，几个圆场可以表示远近不同的场景变换。大体上说，京戏是使用着写意的表演手段的，但也并不排除，有时甚至刻意使用绝对的写实手段，极为细腻地进行刻画、描摹。这正像画家运用大笔泼墨的手法，写出花木、山水，看起来是"逸笔草草"，却又在枝头叶下添写了极精美写实的工笔草虫，跃跃欲动，使画面溢满了生趣。舞台与画案，在这里无疑是息息相通的。

这样，在京剧舞台上就时时可以遇见上好的、精妙绝伦的、有如上佳的短篇小说那样的场合，使人不能不设法将这些舞台上的奇妙光影转移到纸面上来，使之永存，不致退色。这就是这些短章产生的初意，并以之呈献给喜爱中国舞台艺术的异国友人，作为一份微薄的礼物，希望读者能喜欢它。

黄裳

二〇〇六年四月七日

As a result of the cross pollination or interpenetration of the art forms of a nation, there is a similarity between the style of Beijing Opera performances and the minimalist, impressionistic school of Chinese traditional painting. This minimalism is best illustrated by the fact that on the stage a few soldiers are used to represent hundreds of thousands of troops and a few circles made on stage by the actors represent a complete change of scene. Beijing opera is performed as a rule in a minimalist manner but there are exceptions to this rule: detailed, realistic portrayals are sometimes employed, just as in a minimalist splashed-ink landscape or flower-and-bird painting the painter would enliven it by adding laboriously and painstakingly executed, life-like plants, or animals among the leafage. This is a perfect example of the mutual influence between the actor's stage and the painter's canvas.

The stage of Beijing opera so abounds in exquisite scenes that one might liken them to memorable short stories that one feels compelled to preserve forever against fading. The short synopses in this book were written in this spirit and as a gift to people in other countries who have a passion for China's stage art. I hope they will delight my readers.

Huang Shang

7 April 2006

金殿

秦王朝（221BC—206BC）是中国历史上第一个中央集权的大一统的国家，但前后只持续了十四年。秦始皇统治了十二年，接替他皇位的秦二世胡亥昏庸而放荡，在位仅两年，秦王朝就灭亡了。秦始皇去世时，胡亥在奸相赵高的帮助下夺取了皇位。

艳容是奸相赵高的女儿，貌美且聪慧。秦二世爱上了她。但艳容鄙视秦二世，为逃脱沦为秦二世玩物的命运，赵女不得不装疯。

——编者

秦二世的宰相赵高坐在书房里修本，女儿赵艳容陪坐一旁为老父磨墨伸纸。房里静悄悄的，月光透过纱窗在墙上映出了一树老梅的婆娑枝干。父女两人没有话，只听得墨锭在砚底磨出沙沙声音，单调而寂寞。

赵艳容穿着黑色的丧服，神情严肃而悲苦。不施脂粉的面

Golden Palace

The Qin dynasty(221BC-206BC), the first in Chinese history to unite the nation's numerous warring states into one cohesive empire, only lasted for 14 years. The capable but despotic emperor Qin Shi Huang (First Emperor of Qin) ruled for 12 years, and was succeeded by one of his sons, the muddle-headed and dissipated Qin Ershi (Second Emperor) Hu Hai, who managed to rule for only two years before the empire collapsed. Upon the death of his father, Hu Hai came to power with the aid of the treacherous minister Zhao Gao.

Qin Ershi fell in love with the daughter of Minister Zhao Gao, the comely and intelligent Yanrong, who despised him and therefore had no choice but to feign mental derangement to escape being reduced to the emperor's plaything.

-Ed.-

Zhao Gao, Prime Minister under the Second Emperor of the Qin dynasty, sat in his study writing an official petition. His daughter, Zhao Yanrong, sat by his side grinding ink for him and arranging his writing paper. The room was enveloped in silence; on the wall, the dancing shadow of an old plum tree flittered in the moonlight. Father and daughter said nothing to each other. In fact, the only audible sound was the soft monotonous scraping of the inkstick being rubbed on the inkstone.

Dressed in black mourning clothes, Zhao Yanrong was in a state of profound melancholy. Even without makeup, her

庞依旧散发着妙年少妇的光艳，眉头眼角的哀怨更加重了端庄凄楚。她偷眼向执笔沉思的老父看去，眼光落在胸前垂拂大半苍白了的须髯上面，一时竟产生了难以解释的迷惘。坐在身边的仿佛是位陌生的老人，不再是一直朝夕相依的老父了。

半年以前，为了收买、拉拢朝廷上的对手，把女儿当作政治筹码的是他；拉拢不成，下毒手陷害了女婿全家的也是他；当女儿以年轻寡妇身分回到身边，又发了慈悲给皇帝上书要求赦免女婿一家"罪责"的又是他。三种截然不同的面貌、性格怎能在一个具体的人身上统一起来，这不能不给她带来极大的困惑。

赵高仿佛对女儿满怀愧悔，主动地草下了理想的本章，以他在朝中的权势，年轻的小皇帝对他的信赖，本章是会产生好效果的。赵女好像也多少感到了宽慰，向老父赧然一笑。她已经很久没有笑了。

是老父回心转意了么？是自己又重新获得了人的地位，不再被看做货物、筹码了么？在赵女心中重新升起了希望，也许是奢望，她吃不准。正像在大海里发现了一根草，她祝愿它会化为一棵树，一条船，好载了自己躲开不幸。

这时她看到了窗外有一个影子一闪。

face glowed with the beauty of a young woman in her prime, the sadness in her eyes only adding a sense of dignity to her grief. She glanced over at her father who was totally engrossed in his writing. As her eyes fell upon his long white beard, she was struck with an inexplicable feeling of bewilderment: her father seemed to her like a total stranger; no longer was he the boon companion of a lifetime.

Six months earlier, Zhao Gao had attempted to bribe a minister by offering his son his daughter's hand in marriage. He succeeded in marrying his daughter to this young man, but when the minister refused to cooperate, he lodged false charges against his son-in-law's family and they were all executed. And when his recently widowed daughter returned to live by his side, Zhao Gao, in an extraordinary act of mercy, submitted a petition to the throne requesting a pardon for the family's offences. That these three radically contradictory acts were carried out by a single person left her in a state of extreme perplexity.

It was out of a deep sense of shame that Zhao drafted the petition to the throne. Considering the influence he wielded at court and the trust placed in him by the young emperor, his petition was sure to be effective. Zhao Yanrong's relief was visible, and for the first time in months she smiled at her father.

Had Zhao Gao had another sudden change of heart? Or had Yangrong regained her father's respect and no longer would be treated as a pawn in his political game of chess? Along with this came a ray of hope, but regardless of whether this was well-founded, it was enough to allow her to believe that she would be able to avoid getting into any further trouble.

Suddenly she noticed a shadow flashing by the window.

她没有看清楚，只是一个人影。但她自己却立即被唤出，送回了绣房。她身边的哑奴（一个不会说话的伶俐侍女）告诉她，一面频频比着手势，这影子是个无比尊贵的人物，老爷一看见他就下跪。什么人能使宰相下跪呢？她又被告知，在被发现之前，这个影子已在窗外勾留了许久，窥探了许久了。

猜出这影子是谁是容易的。哑奴告诉她，在她嫁出去的日子里，这个"影子"就开始在家里出现了，还常常在夜里。老爷一定准备了许多好玩的事物，才使他每来都流连到夜半。"影子"一来，老爷就吩咐把人赶开，关起门来，因此哑奴也说不清他们说些什么，玩些什么。

奇怪的是，今天"影子"匆匆而来又匆匆而去，她随即又被唤去书房，看见迎面站着的父亲盯住自己只是笑，匆忙地告诉她，修好的本章已经亲手递给了小皇帝，而且立即得到了他的批准。赵高不说下去，看着女儿只是笑，这笑使她毛骨悚然。这是一对发现了猎物的眼睛，欣赏心爱珍宝的眼睛，这样的眼睛里有火。

"恭禧我儿，贺禧我儿。"赵高说，他的双眼眯得更细，花白胡子簌簌地抖。赵女的心凉了，她明白，不管怎样挣扎，不情愿，自己命定还得是货物、筹码，只是这次遇到了更尊贵

Before she could identify who it was, she was called back to her room. Her maid, a deaf-mute, indicated with sign language that the shadow was a man of great prestige and power, and as soon as Zhao Gao saw him, he kneeled down in obeisance. Who would make her father kneel down? And she was told that the shadow had already stood motionless outside the window of the study for quite some time.

It was not hard to guess who this shadow was. Yanrong's maid told her that while she was away from home during her nuptial proceedings, the shadow had appeared many times at night. Zao Gao must habe prepared a variety of delightful entertainments for this mysterious visitor, who never left until well past midnight. Whenever the shadow arrived, Zhao Gao would order everyone away and shut the doors tightly, so the maid knew nothing of what they said or did.

It came as a great surprise when the shadow appeared briefly at the Zhao home and left in haste that evening. Yanrong was then summoned to her father's presence, and with a big smile on his face he told her how he handed the petition to the emperor in person, and how His Majesty approved its contents at once. Zhao Gao's smile sent an unpleasant chill up his daughter's spine. He was as happy as a hunter who had just bagged a rare prize.

'Congratulations my daughter!' Zhao Gao's joy showed from his eyebrows to the tip of his long white beard. But Zhao Yanrong's heart froze, since she knew that no matter how vigorously she protested, it was her fate to remain a pawn, a piece of merchandise in her father's hands, even though in this 'transaction' the 'customer's' status was much higher than before.

的买主。赵高用宣读诏旨的口气宣布，"明日早朝，送进宫去！"

赵女发现在这个世界上已经再没有亲人，除了身边这个不会说话的侍女。哑奴从她是孩子时就和她作伴，陪她遍历了人生艰险，懂得她最隐秘的心事，哑奴不会说话，可是有时只有她才懂得的手势却能表达丰富的情感。哑奴的聪明有时可以为她解除大大小小许多疑难。

她先是向父亲抗议，明知无效但还是抗议了。

"爹爹你身为当朝首相，怎么，连这羞恶之心你你你都没有了么？"她搬出了从小读过的圣经贤传中最响亮的辞句。赵高哪里听得进这些，更不耐烦与女儿分说。他紧逼着提出了责问。"难道你不遵父命！难道你敢违抗圣旨！"

这是从全部圣经贤传的千言万语中提炼出来的精髓，不容违反的律条。能使一切世俗习惯、道德准则统统化为空话，一下子就能判定辩论是非的律条。

赵女知道身后已再没有了路，如有头脑，如有理智，就再不能屈辱地生存，除非她立即化为狂人。这时她看见了哑奴焦急作出的手势，教她脱下衣服，拔去钗环，抓破头面，

Speaking as if he were delivering an imperial edict at court, he announced, 'Tomorrow morning, it's off to the palace with you!'

Yanrong felt she had no friends in the world except for her maid who had attended Yanrong since she was a child, braving hardships at her side and sharing the deepest secrets of her heart. Though she was incapable of speech, she communicated subtle emotions by means of a set of hand signals which only Yanrong understood. Often it was her maid's cleverness that rescued Yanrong from a whole range of difficult situations.

Though she knew the futility of it, she was determined to protest her father's decision anyway.

'Father, you are a Prime Minister at the imperial court. How could you act with 'a heart so full of shame'?' She began by quoting phrases from the classical books which she had studied ever since she was a little girl. But her father had no patience to debate this matter with her, and sternly rebuked her. 'How dare you disobey your father's instructions? How dare you violate His Majesty's sacred edict?'

These words were the distillation of countless volumes of classical wisdom, and wielded absolute authority in all disputes. In fact, such statements had the power of reducing any appeal to traditional practice or popular morality to a bunch of empty talk.

Yanrong knew she had no way out. As a rational being, she could endure such humiliation no longer. Thus her only choice was to feign madness. With a series of agitated gestures, her maid instructed her to take off her clothing, remove the ornaments from her hair, scratch her face with her nails and

一直倒在地上打滚。是的，只剩下这唯一可行的逃避屈辱的路了。

赵女出乎意料的举动先是使赵高吃惊，继而怀疑，最后默默承认是自己逼疯了亲生的女儿。她亲昵地抓起他的袍角，偎倚在他的身边，先是叫他"儿子"，后来叫他"丈夫"，还要拖他到后房去。赵高懂得这是一个失去丈夫的新婚少妇内心活动的发作。一个正常女人锁在心里的话，她毫无顾忌地说出来了。除了疯狂，不应该有另外的解释。

赵高心中也曾闪过一个作父亲的短暂的悔恨，但立即为更强烈的懊丧心情取代了。他为手中价值连城的资本顿时化为一文不值的废物而深深懊丧、哀叹。

赵高不想甘冒欺君之罪，第二天还是把确信已经发疯了的女儿送上了金殿。

秦二世这个小流氓，一早就坐在金殿上等了。他早已得了报告，他满腹疑团，他不相信昨夜灯下看见的美人一下子竟发了疯，他更不相信他宠信的宰相会欺骗自己。他深信赵高的忠诚，也深信赵高在自己的权势与女儿的贞节之间不会作出错误的判断、选择。

roll around on the floor. This was Yanrong's only escape from a lifetime of shame.

Yanrong 's strange behavior came as a great shock to her father. After some initial suspicion, he began believing that he had driven her to this unfortunate state. Provocatively, she toyed with the hem of his robe and rubbed up against him. At first she teased him by addressing him as her son and then her husband, and even tried to drag him off to her bedroom. Zhao Gao interpreted her behavior as resulting from the emotional frustration of a young widow, and her words as an expression of what normal young women kept locked up in the depths of their hearts. He concluded that her behavior was nothing but sheer madness.

For a moment, a pang of paternal remorse passed through Zhao Gao's heart. But this was replaced quickly by a stronger, longer-lasting sense of disappointment inspired by the decline of his daughter's 'market value' - from that of a priceless relic to that of a piece of junk.

Unwilling to risk bringing displeasure to the emperor, Zhao Gao escorted his stricken daughter to the emperor's Golden Palace the very next day.

The emperor, an out-and-out rogue, had been waiting on the throne from early morning. Naturally, he had been warned of Yanrong's condition, and this had filled him with suspicion: How could the woman whom he had seen the previous evening with his very own eyes have gone mad overnight? And would his most trusted Prime Minister dare to deceive him? The emperor placed great trust in Zhao Gao, and believed that he would not dare err in choosing between his own power at court and his daughter's chastity.

　　坐在宝座上的小流氓紧盯着发了疯的赵女在殿陛前下了凤辇，她盛装着，凤衣斜披在身上，脸上还留着昨夜的爪痕，但却更显得俏丽，跨着不像是女人的步子，反而更大方了。她脸上堆着笑，大步跨上金殿，左右顾盼，向两旁的官员们微笑、招呼；走过用金瓜、斧钺组成的"刀门"时，两只小手一挥，就使武士们后退。

　　哑奴被留在了午门外面，只剩下自己面对张牙舞爪的敌人。这时已不能后退也来不及后退，她定了定神，看见坐在大殿正中的小皇帝和分班站在两侧的大臣们，老父紧靠着宝座，在皇帝耳边说着什么，一面指点着自己，正像商人向主顾介绍自己的货色似的。

　　她每走一步都觉得非常艰难，脚下沉重得很。她必须十分留神，不能露出一点破绽。她没有按朝仪在皇帝面前下拜，只是轻轻道了一声"万福"。

　　反常的行动得到的是正常的理解——讪笑，皇帝和大臣们一起笑了起来。赵女耸起双耳细听朝堂上的反应。猛然一

Seated on the throne, the emperor watched Yanrong as she stepped out of her sedan chair. Her face bore an expression of profound sadness, and she wore a long cape draped over her shoulders. The scratches she had made on her own face the night before were still visible, but to the young emperor this only added to her beauty. And when she began strutting about with rather undainty strides, he thought she was more beautiful than ever. With a broad smile on her lips, she strutted about the court, waving flirtatiously at the officials in attendance. And as she approached the double row of guards, who with their long-handled weapons held out before them formed a "tunnel of blades", every single soldier stepped back to let her pass.

Since her maid was forbidden to enter the palace, Zhao Yanrong had to face the music alone. This was neither the time nor the place to consider making an escape. In front of her sat the young emperor, surrounded by his many ministers. Her father stood at the emperor's side, whispering into his ear and pointing at Yanrong, like a merchant discussing a shipment of goods.

With every step she took, Yanrong felt her body becoming heavier and heavier. She reminded herself that she had to exercise the greatest caution in order not to expose her deception. Though she had not bowed down to the emperor in the proper fashion, she did address him with a brief "Your Majesty."

Her abnormal behavior was met with a rather conventional response. She laughed out loud at the assembled ministers, but they, following the lead of the emperor, merely smiled back. Suddenly she was struck with the realization that she could not

惊，不能停留在这地步，她也拍着手笑起来，在朝堂上打着转，用手指着皇帝，用笑宣泄了一个少女的全部激情。

"你笑我疯癫，我笑你的荒淫无道。"她走了一圈。走到父亲身边，拍拍他，二老哥，列位大人，你们听——

"想先皇当年，东封秦岱，西建咸阳，南收五岭，北造万里长城。指望江山万代，永保平安。不想你这昏王荒淫无道，不理朝纲。这天下乃人人之天下，非你一人之天下，似你这样任用奸佞，沉迷酒色，这天下，你是未必坐得长久哟！"

在那样的时代，那样的场合，只有"疯子"才能自由说出人们深藏在心底的话，也不是每一个"疯子"都能幸运地得到这样的机会。整个大殿里没有一点声音。那些大臣、内侍、武士都像木雕泥塑似的站着，没有谁出来呵斥、打断，人人都偷眼望着赵高，好像只有他才能判决这"疯话"是真理还是谬误。连高坐在宝座上的小流氓也满脸迷惘地看着赵高，

continue in this vein, and began clapping her hands and laughing out loud while running madly about the court room, pointing at the emperor and giggling with the abandon of a little girl.

'You think it's a big joke that I'm insane, don't you? Well, I think it's even more ridiculous that you're nothing but a dissipated old scoundrel!' She continued strolling about in a circle and came up to her father's side. 'Older brother, and members of the court: listen to what I have to say.

"Back when the First Emperor was on the throne, he carried out the sacred sacrifice on Taishan Mountain in the east; he built the city of Xianyang in the west; he conquered the Five Great mountains in the south; and he built the Great Wall in the north. He believed that his empire would last for ten thousand years and that his country would forever remain at peace. What a far cry he was from you, you unprincipled debauched rogue! This world belongs to all people; how can a single individual claim it as his own? The way you surround yourself with corrupt officials and indulge yourself in wine, women and song, how long can you expect to remain on the throne?'

At that time and place, only a madman could get away with making such statements. In fact, few madmen ever had such opportinities presented to them. Throughout the entire throne room, not a single sound could be heard. All those present - the great ministers, the emperor's personal servants and the military guards - stood there like wooden dummies, daring neither to interrupt nor rebuke her. All eyes fell upon Zhao Gao, as if he alone were qualified to judge whether these crazed statements were true or not. Even the emperor seated upon his mighty throne cast a perplexed glance at Zhao Gao, as if to

好像失悔不该逼了赵高把发了疯的女儿送进宫来。赵高埋怨地望了皇帝一眼，没有话。

整个大殿，寂静得没有一点声音。

赵女扯下了头上的凤冠，脱下身上的霞帔，卷作一团，扔在地上。她想，装疯是不能停顿的，疯话也是没有限制的。她在脱在地上的宫装上践踏，发出高兴的笑声。

"若再疯癫，斩头来见！"在皇帝看来，疯病是可以用死的威胁来治疗的。

"哟哟哟！我也不知道这皇帝老官有多大威风，动不动就要斩头来见！"她向上望去，嘻嘻地笑了。说不定这将是最后的笑，那就得笑得畅亮，笑得勇敢，使笑声永远在人间回荡。

"你可知道，一个人的头斩了下来，是还能长得上去的！"

在金殿上表演了好半日，幸而没有露出破绽，她实在感到了非常的疲倦，她再也控制不了自己，最后说出了这句完全清醒的回答。但没有谁听得懂这话里的意思。

赵女终于被赶下了金殿。她拖着沉重的脚步走下了殿阶，浑身几乎没有了半点力气。她看见等在午门外面的哑奴飞也似的奔来，她张开双臂，蹒跚地向前迎去，一下子扑在哑奴怀里，放声地痛哭了。

express his regrets for having pressured him into bringing his daughter to the palace. Zhao Gao glared back at the emperor without saying a word.

The entire room remained absolutely silent.

Yanrong then took off her 'phoenix' headdress, removed her tassled cape, rolled them both up together and threw them on the floor. She knew that when feigning madness, there should be no cutting corners, and no limits imposed on her insane prattle. She began trampling on the gown she had thrown on the floor.

'If you continue like this, I'll have your head chopped off!' the young emperor said. He believed that insanity could be cured with the threat of decapitation.

'Yes, yes, yes! Now we'll see if this great emperor truly dares to cut off my head.' Yanrong lurched forward, laughing as she spoke. She laughed in such a way that no one there would ever forget it; for she knew quite well that this was possibly her last laugh.

'You know, of course, that once you chop off my head, it'll grow right back again.'

She had pulled off this performance without a flaw, but it left her so exhausted that she found it difficult to maintain her self-control. Her final statement was, surprisingly, highly rational, yet not a single person understood what she meant.

Zhao Yanrong finally left the palace. As she dragged herself down the long staircase, she felt as if she would collapse. When she reached the outer gates of the palace, her speechless maid was there to greet her. Falling into her embrace, she broke down in tears.

追信

  刘邦仗三位能人萧何、张良、韩信相助，与众诸侯相争天下得胜，于公元前206年建立了汉朝。

  刘邦起初不识韩信之能，未重用他，只给了他一个小官职。韩信愤而出走。听说韩信离开，萧何立即追赶，当夜将韩信追劝回来。

  多亏韩信出色的军事战略才能，刘邦才得以统一中国，建立了持续四百多年的汉朝。

——编者

  连绵的秋雨一个劲儿地下着，韩信坐在褒城治粟都尉寒伧的公廨大厅上，忽然感到了排挤不开的烦闷。

  褒城是一个土筑的小城，周围不过数里，城墙不及一丈，现在算是汉中王刘邦的驻地。城里只有有数几所像样的房子，给大王和文武百官一分，剩下来留给他这个管粮官的公廨，

The Pursuit of Han Xin

Before he founded the Han dynasty in 206BC, Liu Bang became involved in a conflict with his enemies during which he relied upon the help of three able men Xiao He, Zhang Liang and Han Xin.

Liu Bang was initially unaware of Han Xin's ability and entrusted him with only a minor official post, causing him to quit in anger. Hearing that Han Xin had left, Xiao He immediately pursued him and brought him back that very evening.

Later, thanks to Han Xin's brilliance as a military strategist, Liu Bang was able to unite China and found the Han dynasty, which lasted for more than 400 years.

-Ed.-

The autumn rain pattered on with no signs of letting up. Han Xin, seated in the main hall of the small compound allocated to him as the Director of Provisions in Baocheng, was overwhelmed with a feeling of boredom.

Baocheng was a small city of mud houses with a perimeter of only a few kilometers. Its outer walls were less than three meters high. But now it served as the headquarters of the great King of Hanzhong, Liu Bang. The few decent houses in the city had all been appropriated by the king and his senior officials; what was left to Han Xin, a mere grain officer, was hardly better than a stable. When bored, he would pace the

其实比马厩也好不了多少。韩信闷起来在大堂上闲踱，只十来步就不能不碰壁，折回来，再碰壁，这就更加使他气闷。

褒城城里到处是风沙，全城只有横直两条十字街。韩信没有家小，没有熟人，没有朋友。他渐渐从心底滋长了对这个小城的厌烦。真想不到，有名的美人褒姒就出生在这个土围子里。真是"鸡窝里出了金凤凰"了。驻扎在这个鬼地方的刘邦，好像倒颇沉得住气，每天上朝，问事，发脾气，摆威风，看来日子过得挺充实、满足。韩信想，这人难道真的有成更大气候的希望么？

也不能说韩信没有一个朋友。那个小老头儿、丞相萧何就对他不坏。第一天萧何引韩信上殿参见刘邦，事前就告诉他说，大王是会加以重用的，不料结果只给他当了一名粮库看守。韩信站在殿廷下面，冷眼看刘邦脸上一片木然神色，萧何局促不安连连移换着脚步的情形，心里就明白了大半。好像亲眼看到了萧何推荐自己，遭到刘邦反对，两人中间引起了争论的全部情景，甚至连刘邦对他的评价也猜得出来。

"韩信，这个淮阴出身的小流氓，向漂母讨饭，给无赖钻

floor of the hall but could not take more than a dozen steps before running into the wall, and this only aggravated his frustration.

In the city it was sand, sand everywhere. There were only two roads and a single intersection. Han Xin, who had neither friends nor relatives nor acquaintances there, harbored an intense dislike for the place. He could hardly believe that it was in this shabby 'fortress' that the ancient beauty Bao Si was reputed to have been born; if true, this was, indeed, a case of 'a golden phoenix being born into a chicken's nest', but Liu Bang seemed to tolerate everything about this ghostly place. Day after day he held court, attended to state affairs, put on airs and lost his temper as if life here were normal, full and gratifying. Were there indeed hopes, Han Xin wondered, that this man would do great things someday?

Han Xin had one friend: the little old man, Xiao He, who was Liu Bang's prime minister, was good to him. The day he presented Han Xin to the king, he had consoled him by telling him that the king would use him well. Liu Bang, however, made him the guardian of the grain depot. Standing at the far end of the king's court, Han Xin saw clearly Liu Bang's uninterested look and Xiao He's agitation, which told him more than half the story: Xiao He had recommended him, but Liu Bang had sniffed at the recommendation and a dispute had ensued between the two. He could guess what was Liu Bang's opinion of him.

'Han Xin! That little rascal from Huaiying who asked for alms from a washerwoman and crept between the legs of a

裤裆，我要是重用了这种人，三军怎么能服，诸侯安得不笑？还有那项羽又该说些什么呢？……"

韩信心里清楚，这就是他身上背了多年的"鉴定书"，走来走去几乎没听见任何不同意见。他知道这"鉴定"是错误的，曾寄大希望于刘邦，希望听到他会说出不同的意见。但，失望了。

萧何就两样。好像多少能摸到自己的心，为人也和气，不摆丞相的架子。不过在刘邦面前，他的话好像也并无怎样的分量。那毛病怕就在废话多，年纪不大就唠唠叨叨像个老头儿了。

韩信一眼就看出刘邦也是个流氓。在流氓面前，废话是不起作用的。也就为了这，他身上虽然藏着张良的介绍信，但至今并不摸出。他明白，在流氓那里，介绍信（即使是张良出的）也不是能起决定作用的事物。

韩信想起了他在项羽帐下当执戟郎官时的事。项羽不是流氓，是饭桶，这是明明白白的。饭桶并不可怕，倒是他身边的范增是个并不糊涂的老精怪，他了解自己，他向项羽建议，对有能力的人，或重用或杀掉，不能迟疑。这就是他从

scoundrel. If I gave him a high position, would my armies obey me any more? Wouldn't the princes and dukes laugh at me? And what would Xiang Yu say?'

Han Xin was well aware of the stigma he had carried with him all these years. Wherever he went, he had heard nothing different about him. He knew the stigma was wrong and had pinned his hopes on Liu Bang, from whom he expected to hear something different. It was a bitter disappointment.

Xiao He was different from Liu Bang. It seemed that he understood Han Xin's feelings to a certain degree. He was also very polite, possessing none of the overbearing qualities of a prime minister; only his words seemed to carry little weight with the king. Possibly the trouble was that he tended to talk too much. Though not really advanced in years, he would, when talking, rattle on endlessly like an old man.

Han Xin saw at once that Liu Bang was a rascal on whom it was useless to waste words. That was why he had not presented Zhang Liang's letter of recommendation which he had concealed on his person. He was sure that the letter, even though it was from such a prestigious person as Zhang Liang, could have no positive effect on a rascal.

Now sitting alone in his residence, he reflected on the days when he was a halberd-bearer in Xiang Yu's camp. It was quite clear to him that Xiang Yu was not a rascal, only a good-for-nothing whom he had no need to fear. But Xiang Yu's man Fan Zeng was an out-and-out rascal and in no way muddle-headed. He knew Han Xin's ability and had suggested to his master that a clever man must be used well or put out of the way; there was no room for hesitation. That was why he had fled Xiang Yu's

项羽帐下逃走来到褒城的原因。想到这里，他不禁感到目前处境的危险了。

韩信看看身边，一个小小的行李卷，一柄宝剑，真是别无长物。要走，只要拍拍屁股就可以拔脚。公案上是一叠账册，一颗关防，一盏菜油灯。韩信下了决心，提了小包，背上剑，从马房里牵出一匹官马，纵身跳上，向东城驰去，出城时还向守关的令尹快乐地打了一个手势。

"是下乡催粮去么？好走，好走。"

萧何是细心人，也是个善良的人。他当然不是流氓，不过对流氓的心思、手段却摸得烂熟。

萧何是参预中枢机密的核心人物之一。刘邦在褒城住下来很久了。早就坐立不安。是萧何劝他要耐心，装出打算当一辈子汉中王的神气。萧何还说，想进一步取天下，只靠这几个身边人是不够的，还缺少一员超群的统帅人才。

刘邦接受了萧何的建议，把自己打扮成一个心满意足快活的汉中王，又派出张良寻访兴汉灭楚的元帅，凭介绍信前来投效，只是在韩信身上两人发生了分歧。

camp and come to Baocheng. And when he thought this over again, he began to realize the dangers of his present position.

He looked about him: there was only a small bedroll and a sword. If he wanted, he could leave at once. On his desk were only a stack of account books, an official seal and an oil lamp. His mind was made up. Picking up the bedroll and buckling on his sword, he went out to the stable, mounted one of the official steeds, and headed for the east gate. As he passed through it, he waved jovially to the officer on guard.

'Off to the countryside to get grain? Have a safe journey!' shouted the officer.

Xiao He was both cautious and kindhearted. He was not a rascal of course, but knew well a rascal's way of thinking and doing things.

He was one of Liu Bang's key confidants. When Liu Bang became restless after staying in Baocheng for a time, it was he who counseled him to be patient and to pretend he was content to rule over tiny Hanzhong for the rest of his life. He had also advised the king that if he wanted to seize the whole country someday, it was not enough to rely on his present handful of followers. What he needed was a man of genius like his commander-in-chief.

Taking Xiao He's advice, Liu Bang behaved like a contented King of Hanzhong and at the same time secretly sent out Zhang Liang to find some worthy commander who could help him conquer Chu (Xiang Yu's kingdom) and establish the Han dynasty. This man was to come to him with Zhang Liang's letter of recommendation. Unfortunately, a difference arose between Liu Bang and Xiao He in their estimate of Han Xin's ability.

萧何陷入了两面夹攻的困境。他一方面要花大力气说服刘邦，重用韩信，费尽唇舌给韩信提升了一级，这是使人失望的，破格录用的可能看来没有了；在韩信那里，萧何就要反复说明一切得慢慢来的道理，同时还得为刘邦解释，说他到底还是一个明白人。

不过这两条都很难说得清楚。韩信是聪明人，花言巧语在他那里是无用的，何况，又很有几次对萧何的唠叨表示了不耐烦，这就使这位丞相感到说不出的为难。

萧何天不亮就起了床，站到院子里眯着眼望天。一连下了几天的秋雨终于放晴了，竟是满天星斗。这就使他高兴起来，不停地搓着双手，嘴里喃喃地说着什么。其实身边并没有人，他只是对自己反复地说，"应该去望望韩信了。"丞相跑到粮官的公廨去，是失身份的，不过萧何已先后去过几次了。

萧何大声地喊院公套车。叫了几声无人应。萧何心想也许是门房离得远，听不见，就又接着喊。一会，那院公踉踉跄跄地奔进来了，一脸惊慌。

"韩将军弃官逃走了！"

Xiao He found himself beset with diffculties on both sides. On the one hand, he had done everything he could to persuade the king to give Han Xin an important post, but had only succeeded in having him promoted by one grade. It was most disappointing and there seemed to be no hope of promoting him over the heads of the king's other officers. On the other hand, he had to convince Han Xin of the need to be patient; he had to speak out for his master, trying to make Han Xin believe that the king, after all, was a sensible person.

Both tasks were difficult. Han Xin was a clever man and it was no use flattering him; on several occasions he had shown his displeasure at Xiao He's long-windedness. The prime minister was, indeed, in a tough spot.

Xiao He was up before dawn. He stood in the courtyard with his eyes half-closed, looking upwards. The sky was full of stars, for the rain that had continued for days had finally ended. This livened up his spirits somewhat and as he rubbed his hands briskly, he kept muttering something under his breath. There was no one nearby. He was merely talking to himself, repeating over and over: 'I've got to go and see Han Xin.' Though it was below the dignity of a prime minister to call on a grain officer, Xiao He had done this a number of times.

He called out to the gatekeeper to harness his carriage, but there was no response. Assuming that it was because the gatehouse was too far away and his orders had not been heard, he called again. In a short while, the keeper came limping up with a frightened look on his face:

'General Han has fled!'

"有谁见来？"

"东门令尹前日见他下乡催粮，至今未归。"

听了此言，萧何忘却了相爷的身分，也忘记了自己的年纪，他平日细心，但这回却再不想过细盘问了，这一定是真的，是他早就料到了的。只不过来得太快了一些。他迈着碎步在院子里走着，只简单地询问了韩信穿的什么，可带了家私？就连声吩咐备马。

"相爷，你骑得马么？平日都是套车。"院公迟疑着。

"糊涂东西！快备马！"萧何真的控制不住自己了。

一会子院公牵来了两匹马，后面跟着一名壮健的亲军。萧何穿着长袍、靴子，扶掖着好不容易爬上马背，认镫也困难，还是院公将靴子塞了进去的。

萧何在马背上摇摇的。迎面一阵秋风，帽子几乎被吹掉，用手一按时，帽沿就倾斜地压住了眉梢。萧何两眼直直的，打了一鞭，马儿就像箭似的窜出了府门。

街上是一片烂泥。马蹄过处，大片泥浆就向两旁飞去，行人都远远躲在房檐下面，露着惊奇的脸色望着骑马的人。直挺挺坐在马背上的萧何，正像是驮着的一块门板。

'Who told you?'

'The officer guarding the east gate saw him leave for the country to collect grain. That was two days ago and he hasn't returned yet.'

On hearing this, Xiao He set aside the dignity of a prime minister as well as his own years. Usually a careful man, he did not care to ask much this time; the news must be true, for he had long anticipated it, though not as soon as this. He paced the courtyard in quick steps, enquired briefly about Han Xin's clothes and whether he had taken his personal belongings, and then gave orders to saddle his horse.

'Can Your Excellency ride a horse? You always travel by carriage,' asked the keeper skeptically.

'Fool! Hurry up and ready my horse!' Xiao He had lost control of himself.

The keeper led two horses over, followed by a sturdy bodyguard. Xiao He in his long robes and high boots was helped into the saddle with some difficulty. He had a hard time finding the stirrups and the keeper had to squeeze his boots into them.

As he sat shakily in the saddle, a gust of wind nearly blew off his hat. He pressed it down and the brim covered his eyebrows. With his eyes fixed straight ahead, he gave his steed a tap with the whip and it sped like an arrow out of the front gate.

The streets were full of mud, which the flying hooves of the horses splashed in all directions, forcing passers-by to take shelter under the nearest eaves. From there they watched the two riders, especially Xiao He who sat bolt upright.

马背上的萧何这时正转着与范增差不多的念头。他们信奉的正是同样的原则。人才自然以聚在自己手下为好，多多益善；如果留不住，那就宁可杀掉。如果让他跑到敌人一边去，那可是天大的灾祸。

他们站在敌对的阵营里进行了百十次大小规模的厮杀，从实践经验中获得了相同的结论。不过萧何比范增乐观得多，他相信韩信是可以追回来的，因而不必杀掉，还能受到大大的重用。他的主要根据是：从根本上说来，刘邦和项羽是不同的。

出了东门以后，眼前就是一条小路蜿蜒着通向山里，此外别无路径。宿雨初晴，小路上还留下了杂沓却是清晰的马蹄痕迹，萧何用力抽打马儿的屁股，使它没命地狂奔起来。发怒的马在小路转折处摆脱了背上的负担，兀自悠闲地啮起了路边碧绿的野草。亲军赶到时，发现相爷正倚着一棵大树喘息，身上的锦袍一半已浸透了泥水。

亲军搀了萧何重新跨上马背，又赶了好半日，一直走到太阳正中，人困马乏，又饥又渴，忽发现前面崖角丛绿里飞

The thoughts that turned in Xiao He's mind as he rode along were much the same as those of Fan Zeng, for there was one principle in which both men believed. Talented people should be won over to one's own side, the more the better; but if that could not be done, the next best thing was to dismiss them because it would be disastrous if they went over to the enemy.

He and Fan Zeng had served in rival camps that had fought each other hundreds of times, and it was through long, hard experience that they arrived at this truth. But Xiao He was more optimistic: he was sure be could get Han Xin back, so there was no need to plan his death; the man could still be put to great use. His reasoning was based on an understanding that Liu Bang and Xiang Yu were radically different persons.

After passing through the east gate, they saw before them a series of low hills with a single narrow path winding through them. Notwithstanding the rain, which had ceased only a short while ago, the marks of horse hooves could be seen clearly. Xiao He gave his horse a few hard kicks and it bolted forward. At a sharp turning in the road, the furious beast threw off its rider and trotted away to nibble at the green grass at the roadside. When the guard rode up, he found the prime minister leaning against a large tree, his brocade robes already half soaked with muddy water.

The guard helped him into the saddle again and they rode on for another half day. It was high noon now and both men and horses were exhausted, hungry and thirsty. Not far in front they spotted a cliff, at the foot of which was a thick

下一条小小的瀑布，宛如一挂珠帘，不必说下面必有一处深潭。这时又传来了一声长长的马嘶，紧行几步，看到韩信就坐在那里歇息，战马缚在潭边老树身上。

三人一起站着不动，彼此打量了好半日。

韩信见相国那种狼狈相，不禁失笑，一切不必说也自然清楚了。

"你急的什么！我正要找你去，却听说你跑了。这成什么话，一切都会好起来的，我又跟大王说过了，……"韩信听任萧何唠叨，只是笑。

"等见了刘邦，再把张良的介绍信取出来吧。"韩信想，"没有介绍信，空口白话，看来他还是不相信……"

三匹马在归途上慢慢地走着，泥泞的小路已经干了。

growth of greenery with a small cascade that hung there like a pearled curtain. There must be a deep pool beneath it, which was just what they needed. The neighing of a horse broke the silence. They hurried on a few more steps and there, sitting beside the pool, his horse tied to an old tree nearby, was the object of their pursuit.

The three stood there motionless, eyeing each other for some time.

Seeing the prime minister's sorry appearance, Han Xin could not help laughing. There was no need for words; everything was clear.

'What's the hurry! I was just going to call on you when they told me you had run away. How could you! Everything'll be all right; I've spoken to the king again...' Xiao He rattled on, but Han Xin only listened with a smile.

'I'll take out Zhang Liang's letter when I see Liu Bang,' Han Xin thought to himself. 'Looks like he won't take me at my word without a letter of recommendation.'

The three horses trotted leisurely back over the small muddy path, which by then had dried up.

痴梦

　　本剧讲述朱买臣之妻崔氏嫌丈夫家贫，逼其休了自己改嫁他人。后来，朱买臣中试当上太守，崔氏十分后悔。一天晚上，她做了一个梦，梦里自己仍是前夫朱买臣之妻，有人给她送来了官诰服装：凤冠霞披。欣喜之中，她见到现夫突然手持利斧出现了。她猛然惊吓醒来，环视周围，只悲哀地看见破墙断垣。

　　历史上确有朱买臣（？—115BC）其人，他是汉武帝时的一位官员，业绩平凡，并无大名。然而，几乎每一个中国传统剧种都有根据朱买臣休妻的内容改编的剧本，从而使他全国闻名。

——编者

　　这一阵子崔氏吃过午饭总要到自家门口站一会儿。她的心情经常陷入说不出的又宁帖又忐忑的那么一种状态，仿佛时时感到精神恍惚，这是生活突然从费尽心思张罗柴米的困

A Foolish Dream

This opera deals with how Zhu Maichen's wife, Madame Cui, looked down upon him for being poor, and divorced him to marry another. Afterwards, when Zhu Maichen attained rank and power, Madame Cui was filled with regret. One evening she had a dream in which she envisioned that she was still married to her former husband and that someone had been dispatched to present her with a phoenix coronet and a silk cape, the costume of a high official's wife. But in the midst of her delight she imagined that her present husband suddenly appeared with an axe. Awaking in fear, she gazed all around her and felt terribly grieved to see the dilapidated walls of her present surroundings.

Zhu Maichen (?-115 BC), an actual historical figure, was an official during the reign of Emperor Wu Di during the Han dynasty, but his deeds were of little historical importance. However, since almost every genre of Chinese traditional opera features works based on the theme of Zhu Maichen rejecting his former wife, his name is well known throughout China.

-Ed.-

Of late, Madame Cui would always go to the front door and stand there for a while after her midday meal. Very often she would fall into a state of both complacency and uneasiness that was hard to explain, and sometimes she even seemed to be in a trance. It all resulted from a sudden change in her life.

窘状态转入粗茶淡饭的小康局面的结果。这使她一下子觉得忽地闲下来，竟连手脚好像也没处放了。因此她就常常一个人来到门首闲眺。望望那远远葱翠的烂柯山，那从山脚伸出来的崎岖羊肠小路。这时，一幕幕赶也赶不开的往事就会蓦地兜上心来。

她经常是呆呆地望着那山脚，一望就是好半日。她细细回忆，自己是怎样一步一跌地从那条崎岖山路上走下来的。不容易啊！出嫁前父母的嘱咐，"好马不备双鞍，好女不嫁二夫"的社会舆论，曾多少次抑制过她那"非分"的念头！跟只会抱着一本破书的书呆子朱买臣过了那么多年苦难的日子。这个书呆子，就是落到上山砍柴度日的境地还不忘在柴担上放一本书，一面走一面嘴里不住地吟哦。念得出神一交跌在路边的时候也不是没有过。想想这些往事，崔氏不禁又好气又好笑，她长长地叹了口气。到底从这个无指望的家中逃出来了。

她记得开始时也曾相信过朱买臣的话，说从书本里是会读出黄金的屋子和高车驷马、凤冠霞帔、成群的奴婢等等来

Formerly a wife who constantly had to worry about her next meal, she was now sufficiently well off to enjoy simple homely fare all the time, and the change had relieved her of so much housework that she did not know what to do with her hands and feet, as if they were not content to be idle. So she would pass the time at the front door, gazing at the green Lanke Hills in the distance and the winding footpath beneath them, and as she did so, visions of the past rose like dreams, or nightmares, that could not be dispelled.

Quite often she would stare blankly at the foot of the hills for almost half a day, musing on her past, recalling how she had limped down the hill along that narrow path. No, it wasn't easy. Just before her first marriage, her parents had exhorted her to remember the popular saying: 'A good horse will not take a second saddle; a good girl will not marry a second time.' Remembering this, she had time and again suppressed 'inappropriate' ideas and remained faithful through many difficult years to the pedant Zhu Maichen who knew nothing besides reading books. It was this idiotic pedant who, when forced to cut firewood for a living, would place a book upon his load and recite as he walked along, and not infrequently, as a result of being too engrossed, would trip and fall by the roadside. It both amused and vexed her when she recalled these absurdities, but now, at last, she had escaped from that hopeless family. And she heaved a long sigh.

She still remembered that in the beginning she had believed him when he told her that palaces of gold, royal four-horse coaches, phoenix coronets, rosy capes, trains of maidservants ... all would come through reading books. Zhu

的。朱买臣是个好脾气的温柔的丈夫，她偎在丈夫怀里听着
这些对未来的美好描述时，也确曾深深相信并沉醉过。朱买
臣是个老实人，不像是个红口白舌吹牛说大话的汉子，这一
点到今天她还是相信的。只怪他给鬼迷了心窍，他是真心实
意的相信着这一切的，并非挖空心思编造出来欺骗自己可爱
可怜的妻子。可是她终于"悟"出，这一切都是神话，是不
可能实现的梦。当然，邻居女人的议论也是起了不小作用的。
"年轻轻的，花朵似的人儿，跟着这疯疯癫癫的书呆子，到那
一天才是个了局。别听那些胡言乱语了，几时看到顶马官轿
抬进过这山沟里来！"

　　每想到这一切，崔氏心里总是软软的，伴着轻微的痛楚。
书呆子当然并不可爱。可是比起现在嫁的这个丈夫来，到底
是不同的。她现在想的是吃穿不愁，可是失去的是什么呢？
她说不清楚。她一直在掂量着自己采取这断然举措的得失。
不过这是一笔无力算清的帐。

　　她并不后悔，可是也不能没有丝毫负疚的心情。尤其是
她最后下狠心逼着朱买臣写下休书的那个夜晚。事后想起都
有些后怕。她果真是这样一个狠心辣手的女人么？这一切都
是邻居女人帮她策划的，"只有这一招了，要不你就死心塌地
地跟他一块饿死，冻死！"

was a kind and good-tempered husband. As she lay in his arms and listened to his beautiful tales of the future, she not only believed it all, but was quite enchanted. Even now she saw him not as a braggart, but as an honest man. If he was to be blamed, it was only because he himself, like one possessed, also believed his stories and was not trying to deceive his beloved but miserable wife. In time, however, she 'realized' that they were mere fantasies, dreams that would never come true. Of course, the gossip of the women in the neighborhood also had an effect on her. 'Such a young girl, and as pretty as a flower. How long will you go on living with that half-crazy book worm? Don't be taken in by all that nonsense. When will noble horses and sedans ever come to this poor valley?'

When she reflected on all this now, Madame Cui's heart would soften with a slight compunction. The pedant was not a likable person, to be sure, but he was different from her present husband. What she had gained from the change was security from cold and hunger, but what was it that she had lost? She could not say even though she had been weighing the consequences of the decisive step she had taken. It was a piece of reckoning that could not be made clear.

Though she did not regret the step, she could not help harboring a slight feeling of guilt, especially over the events of the last night when she finally hardened her heart and forced her husband into signing the divorce papers. She shuddered whenever she thought of it. Was she really such a mean person? It had all been planned with the help of the woman who lived next door: 'This is your only way out; otherwise you'll just have to stick to him and die together of hunger or cold!'

那天夜里她咬咬牙使出了这最后一招。朱买臣的眼睛都直了。她把笔塞到他手里逼他在休书上画押时，他的手发抖，仿佛教孩子描红似的，是她手把手逼他画了押。随后她就冷不防把休书抢过来，塞进怀里。朱买臣像一堆泥似的瘫倒在那里，没有表情，没有声音。空房里只留下她转身离去的冷笑。

想到这里，她总不禁要打个寒噤。她多少次下决心不再去想这一幕，可是每次最先钻进心来的总是它。

她把发呆的眼神从山脚移过来，移到大路边，和过路的新邻居招呼。这些女人脸上倒都堆着笑，可不知怎的，笑声里好像总夹杂着一点恶意。无聊！她想回家去了。

她刚要推门时，被身后两个公差模样的人唤住了。他们的口气却来得意外的和善，称她"大娘子"。他们是问路的，要打听一位新任本郡会稽太守的家，去报喜。希奇！会稽郡的太守官大着呢，手下管着多少县，怎么不上大县城去找，偏偏钻到这山窝子来。

"这位朱老爷家不知住在哪里？"

崔氏听了心里一动，"哪位朱老爷？"

That fateful night, gritting her teeth, she decided to resort to this last measure. Her poor husband was stupefied. When she thrust a brush into his hand and bade him sign the paper, his hand shook like that of a child ordered by a stern teacher to trace characters in a copybook. She forced him to sign his name, stroke by stroke, and then snatched the paper away and thrust it in her bosom. Zhu collapsed like a heap of clay, speechless and expressionless. The only sound in the room at the time was the sneering laughter of the woman as she turned and walked away.

When she recalled that scene now, a cold shiver ran down her back. She vowed many times never to think of it again; yet always in her pensive moods it was the first to reappear in her mind.

She turned her dreamy eyes from the foot of the distant hills to the main road and hailed some of her new neighbors who were passing by. These women all smiled at her to be sure, but somehow she sensed a bit of malice behind those smiles. A silly notion! She decided to go back into the house.

As she pushed open the door, two men dressed like public servants called to her from behind in voices that were unusually courteous. They addressed her as 'Aunt' and asked the way to the newly appointed Prefect of Kuaiji to offer their congratulations. It sounded a little strange. The Prefect of Kuaiji was a high-ranking offcial governing several counties. Why did these people come all the way to this small valley to look for him instead of going to some large town?

'Where does His Lordship Zhu live?' they asked.

Madame Cui's heart skipped a beat: 'What Lordship Zhu?'

"就是朱买臣，朱老爷。"

"喔，是他么？"崔氏觉得一阵昏眩，怀疑该不是做梦。两个公人看她像是知情，又施了一礼，说，"还望大娘子指引。"

崔氏转过身来手指着远处的烂柯山，只是点头，半晌也挣不出一句话来。

"朱老爷，他，他，就住在那座山下面。"她费了好大力气才用这句话把公差打发上路。

崔氏从厨下端出了饭菜。坐下来，坐了一会子。又收拾了，竟忘却去动筷子。她剔了灯，收拾了衾枕，在床边坐下，却不去解衣。她觉得疲倦极了，想睡下，可是时间还早。只是这样呆坐着也不是事。这时墙角的蟋蟀一阵阵叫起来了，叫得人心慌。

崔氏双眼随着灯焰移动。她在听，街上的人声慢慢沉寂下去了。隔壁人家关了门，上了门杠。再下去就再也听不见一点人声，只有蟋蟀还在叫。

难道这一切都是真的么？公差找到那书呆子了么？找不到就该再回来向她打听，找到了就不会来了。她失悔为什么不把公差让进家里坐，请他们吃茶，告诉他们住在这里的就

'Zhu Maichen, His Lordship Zhu.'

'He?' Madame Cui felt a sudden dizziness and wondered if she were not dreaming. As her manner suggested that she knew something, the men greeted her again and asked, 'Lady, do you know where he lives?'

She turned and pointed towards the Lanke Hills, but could only nod her head continually, seeming to have lost her voice.

Finally, after some effort, she stammered out, 'His Lordship Zhu ... He ... he lives at the foot of those hills,' and with these words she sent them aweay.

Alone in the house, she took out bowls of rice and vegetables from the kitchen cupboard and sat down to supper. After sitting there a while, she put them away again, forgetting that she had not yet taken a mouthful. Next she lit the lamp, rolled out the bedding and sat down beside the bed but did not undress. She felt very tired and wanted to sleep, but it was still too early. And it wouldn't do just to sit there doing nothing. The crickets in the corner began singing and this only added to her annoyance.

Her eyes moved with the flicker of the oil lamp. She was listening attentively. The sounds in the streets gradually died down. One after another her neighbors closed and bolted their doors. Soon there were no more human sounds or voices anywhere, only the singing of the crickets in the wall.

Could it all be true? Did those men find that pedant? If they didn't, they should come back and ask again; but if they did, she would hear from them no more. How she regretted that she had not asked the two men in for a cup of tea and told them that the prefect's wife lived right here ... Why not?

是新太守的夫人……我能这么说么？怎么不能！朱买臣又没听说另讨了家小。自己离开朱家也只不过有数的日子。

今天蟋蟀叫得也有些特别。也许是平常听惯了不留意，细听时，却是有节奏、有韵律的。猛地，灯盏里结了个大灯花，爆了，撒开来，铺开一片火星，在她面前展开了一片灿烂光明。

是谁？门敲得那么急！也许是两个公人回来了。崔氏忙不迭地跳下床，三步两步去开了门。不只是两个公人，后面还跟着一大群。院子、衙婆、七八个皂隶，手里都捧着大红漆盘。崔氏正迟疑时，院子、衙婆早跪下去了，使得她也跪了下去，但立即被扶起，被扶在座上坐了。皂隶们一连串拜了下去，红漆盘都高高举过了头顶。

"我等奉了朱老爷之命，特来迎接夫人上任。"

崔氏定了定神，呆呆地望着跪在地下的一群。身子被扶得定定的，半点移动不得。她在想，这可好了。要紧的是不能错了太守夫人的身分，给老爷丢了面子。刚才院子、衙婆见礼时她竟也跪了一跪，就简直要不得。可是太守夫人到底

After all, she had left Zhu Maichen's house only a short time ago and, as far as she knew, he had not remarried.

The singing of the crickets sounded a little strange tonight. Maybe she had not noticed it before since she had heard it too often, but now as she listened carefully, there seemed to be both rhyme and rhythm to the singing. All of a sudden a large piece of snuff formed in the wick of the lamp; it charred and the sparks it gave off turned into a bright flash ...

Who was that knocking so impatiently at the door? Had the two officials come back? Madame Cui jumped out of bed and hurried over to open the door. Yes, it was those two officials, but they were not alone. Behind them was a train of *yamen* servants, including a woman, and seven or eight runners each holding a large tray of red lacquer. As she stood there not knowing what to do, the servants all knelt down reverently, which shocked her so much that she, too, dropped on her knees. But the woman-servant immediately helped her to her feet and escorted her to a chair. The runners now knelt down one by one and held the red lacquer trays above their heads.

"We are here on the orders of His Lordship to escort Your Lady to your post."

Madame Cui calmed herself as she looked down upon the kneeling party. She held her body stiffly without moving a muscle; for in her mind now the most important thing was not to lose the dignity of a prefect's wife and bring disgrace on His Lordship. Just when the servants were paying their respects, it was a terrible thing for her to fall on her knees, too. But then, what exactly were the properties of a prefect's

应有怎样一套言谈举止，心里却半点也没有谱。不由得又怪起书呆子来，为什么不自己来接呢？

"那朱老爷……"

"朱老爷奉了皇命，星夜赴任去了，临行特派小人等来接夫人随后赶去。"不等她把话说完，院公就说清了原委。这时衙婆站起来，取过皂隶手中的红漆盘，凑将过来。

"夫人，现有凤冠、霞帔在此。"仿佛这就是他们此来的信物。一片银光照得她眼花。一颗颗晶莹耀目的珍珠镶嵌在金银翠贴的冠顶。崔氏只从戏台底下遥遥地望见过这东西，朱买臣倒是告诉过她这凤冠的形制，可惜被她一顿抢白打断了。想到这里，她真觉得有点歉然。到底是知疼着热的丈夫，竟把这凤冠送到她面前来了。

正当崔氏呆呆地出神，院公作了一个手势，几个皂隶取出了随身的乐器，吹弹起来，吓了她一跳。衙婆随手取过凤冠，端端正正地给她戴了。又款款地扶她立起身来。顺手又把霞帔披在她身上。这是大红锦缎、平金绣了海水锦鸡纹样的。衙婆扶着她走了两步，她只觉得有点眩晕，摇摇地步子

wife? She had no idea. Instinctively, she began blaming that pedant for not coming here to fetch her himself.

'His Lordship Zhu ...'

'His Lordship, on the orders of the Emperor, has hurried away to assume his new post. Before he left, he sent your humble servants here to escort Your Lady to his place,' interrupted the head servant. The woman-servant now stood up, took over the red tray from one of the runners and walked up to her.

'Lady, here is the phoenix coronet and rosy cape!' she said as if these were the tokens of their mission. Her eyes were dazzled by their brilliance - the glittering pearls set in a crown of gold, silver and jade. In the past she had only seen such things on the stage while sitting far away in the stalls. Occasionally, Zhu Maichen had described to her the shape and make-up of a coronet; but, unfortunately, she had always interrupted him. She felt some guilt when she thought about it now. He was a loving, warm-hearted husband after all to have sent her this coronet.

As she sat there as if in a trance, the head servant made a gesture, at which the runners took out musical instruments and began playing on them. It frightened her a bit at first. The woman-servant who was standing by picked up the coronet and placed it squarely upon her head, then with great courtesy helped her to her feet and wrapped the cape round her shoulders. It was a piece of bright red brocade with a pattern of the sea and with pheasants embroidered in gold. Supported by the woman, she took a few unsteady steps, feeling somewhat dizzy. She was moving to the music of drums and

都走不稳。在鼓乐声中移步，俯视身前，只见一片耀目的大红。她眯起了眼睛，嘴边漾出一丝平安、愉悦的微笑。她想，自从嫁到朱家以后，还从未这样安舒地笑过。这是从心底迸出来的笑啊！这是没有声音，但却一阵阵使内心产生震颤的笑。

她真的想睡了。本已感到极度疲劳的崔氏，又经过一番折腾，就再也支撑不住，竟自身不由己伏在案上。又不知过多久，在官轿里走了很远的路，最后终于到了太守的官衙。一声号炮，两扇厚重的黑漆大门打开，轧轧地响。她望见穿了大红官衣的朱买臣笑嘻嘻地从大堂上走了下来。她心里慌得很，想快些下轿。不留神，一下子碰到轿门的横杠上。

案上的残灯又爆了好大一个灯花，接着灯光就暗了下来。崔氏怔怔的，什么都没有了，院子、衙婆、皂隶、轿夫、凤冠、霞帔、……连同笑嘻嘻穿着大红锦袍的朱买臣，通通没有了。

鼓乐声也没有了，只有蟋蟀似乎叫得更加起劲。从破墙高处漏进了半轮圆月，皎洁的银光照得满屋亮堂堂的。

flutes, and as she did so she looked down and saw only an expanse of red whose brilliance nearly blinded her. She blinked and slowly let out a smile of pleasure and satisfaction. Never, she thought, since she was married into the Zhu family, had she smiled so contentedly - it was a smile from the bottom of her heart, a smile with reverberations deep within.

Now she really needed some sleep. She had felt totally exhausted before it happened, and now after all this excitement she lost control of herself and collapsed upon the table. A very long time seemed to have passed. Seated in the official sedan-chair, she was carried a long, long way before she finally reached the prefect's residence. Amid an explosion of fireworks, the two heavy black lacquered gates swung open with a loud squeak and there was Zhu Maichen, in his red official robes, smiling at her as he walked out of the main hall. She was nervous and in a hurry to step out of the sedan. In doing so, however, she knocked her head against the lintel above the door ...

Another large piece of snuff flared up in the wick of the lamp and the room gradually darkened. Madame Cui was seized with terror. Everything was gone - the *yamen* servants and runners, the sedan carriers, the phoexix coronet, the rosy cape ... even the smiling Zhu Maichen in his red robes.

The music was gone, too. There was only the singing of the crickets, which sounded louder and harsher than ever. A half-moon rose above the broken garden wall, its beams illuminating the room with a silvery light.

捉放曹

东汉（25—220）末年，朝中大权落入奸臣董卓手中。年轻的曹操刺杀董卓未遂逃走，途经中牟县时为县令陈宫擒获。

出于对曹操行为的同情，陈宫放走曹操，并决定弃官与之同逃。

在中国传统戏剧和小说中，曹操一直被描绘为背信弃义的典型。

——编者

曹操纵马在官道上跑，一只兔子猛地从马蹄前横穿而过，钻进荒草堆里去了。曹操一紧缰绳，收住马，嘴里骂了声"鬼东西！"停下来歇气。豫北平原冬天的傍晚，满眼黄土坡地上长着野草，几乎没有树木，只远远有一小片疏林，一轮落日挂在林梢，苍白、毫无血色，就像一个浮肿病人的脸盘。曹操在马上四望，看不见一个活物，他嘘了一口气，又望见骑在马上跟上来的陈宫拼命抽着鞭子，却依然跑不快。摇摇的

The Capture and Release
of Cao Cao

Towards the end of the Eastern Han dynasty (25-220), power at court fell into the hands of a wicked official, Dong Zhuo. When his attempt on Dong Zhuo's life failed, the young Cao Cao fled, and was arrested as he passed through Zhongmou County by Chen Gong, the county magistrate.

Out of sympathy for Cao Cao's actions, Chen Gong set Cao Cao free, and decided to join him on his flight.

In traditional Chinese drama and fiction, Cao Cao is portrayed as the epitome of undisguised treachery.

-Ed.-

As Cao Cao galloped down the road, a rabbit suddenly darted across the horse's path and plunged into the wild grass at the roadside. Cao Cao reigned his horse to a halt, cursed the 'little demon', and stopped for a rest. On this winter evening in northen Henan Province, the grassy yellow-earth plains stretched nearly treeless as far as the eye could see. Far off in the distance was a sparse copse, with the setting sun hanging above the trees, white and bloodless like the face of an invalid. Looking around him, Cao Cao could see no sign of life and sighed. He then turned to watch the approach of Chen Gong, who was whipping his horse with all his might, yet still unable to speed the animal along. Chen appeared as

一个蓝色小点向前蠕动着，越来变得越大。叹了口气，带着
这么一位书呆子逃亡，可真是个累赘。曹操脸上两道长侵入
鬓的剑眉慢慢拧紧，在眉心结成了一团。覆满风尘的脸没有
一点血色，只在颧骨周围漾出两圈微红。微带棱角的双眼，倒
依旧烁烁有光，机警、闪烁，坚定、凌厉。

　　曹操想，等自己手里有了队伍，能放手干一番事业时，陈
公台（宫）该是一位出色的军师、幕府人才。他骑不来马，就
给他弄一顶轿子，可是眼前两个亡命的光杆，绑在了一起，两
人三条腿……曹操从心里感激陈宫、尊敬陈宫。他在中牟县
落了网，三言两语竟自说服了这位县太爷，不但放了他，还
跟着一起逃亡。天底下哪里去找这样的好人、义士、傻瓜！
他几次压下了扔下他独自逃生的念头，觉得这真是一种羞
耻！这时，曹操就大声地向地上吐一口唾沫。

　　陈宫好容易赶上来了，张着嘴吐气，两手紧紧地拉住缰
绳，睁大了眼睛望着曹操。他们并辔而行了。

　　"前边树林后面，也许是一座庄院。"陈宫说。他们从昨

a small blue dot on the horizon, wriggling back and forth, gradually becoming larger as he approached. Cao Cao sighed again: fleeing with this kind of bookworm in tow was such an encumbrance. Cao Cao frowned, his long slanting eyebrows coming together in the center of his forehead. His dusty face was pale save for two patches of color dotting his cheekbones, but his eyes still held their old sparkle - quick and penetrating, they flashed with determination and vigilance.

Cao Cao mused. When I regain command of my own troops and have more of a free hand to get things done, Chen Gong will be an outstanding adviser, fully worth being my aide-de-camp. Since he's such a poor rider, he can be given a sedan chair ... But what about now? Two fugitive generals fleeing alone, like two men with three legs ... Cao Cao felt the deepest respect and gratitude for Chen Gong. Cao Cao had been captured in Zhongmou County, but with a few words had convinced Chen Gong, the Zhongmou County magistrate, not only to release him, but also to accompany him in flight. Where on earth could one find such a good man, such a righteous man, such a fool! He pushed aside a strong desire to flee on his own, but felt ashamed of himself and spat noisily onto the ground.

Chen Gong finally managed to catch up. Gasping with his mouth open and his hands tightly clutching the reins, he gazed up wide-eyed at Cao Cao. Side by side they rode westwards.

"There's probably a manor house beyond that copse ahead," Chen Gong said. After leaving Zhongmou County the night

夜离开中牟县，一口气跑了整整一天，陈宫实在拖不下去了，但不敢直截了当地提出停下来歇息，只是望着曹操。

"歇息倒是该歇息了，马也跑不动了，只是不知道庄院里住着什么人，是什么路数……"

陈宫不答。他们依旧缓缓地往前走，两匹马不停地把头伸到路边的草窠里，马饿了。

岔路上露出了一个人影。曹操警觉，在马背上伸长了身躯，看清这不过是一个庄户老汉时，才又安下心来坐稳。不料那老汉停下来看了一会大声喊起来：

"孟德，马上可不是孟德吗？"

曹操吃了一惊，脸上变颜变色，示意陈宫催马快走。

"老汉姓吕，昨天晚上令尊还在庄上留宿了一宵，今晨匆匆赶路去了，却不料你这时赶来。"

陈宫老大不愿意，在这种时候碰上一个相识的熟人，可不是好事。但扭不过曹操，还是被老汉让进庄去了。

曹操和陈宫在草堂上对坐。

主人真是好客，强按着他们坐了，吩咐家下人准备酒饭，

before, they had traveled a full day without resting. Chen Gong was on his last legs, but didn't dare propose stopping for a rest, and just gazed at Cao Cao.

'True enough, we need a rest. The horses are exhausted, too . But we don't know if the people who live in the village are friends or enemies.

Chen Gong made no reply. They continued on as before, their horses constantly stretching their necks to graze at either side of the road in an attempt to assuage their hunger.

A figure suddenly came into view on a side road and Cao Cao straightened up in the saddle. Seeing it was only an old villager, he relaxed and sat down again. The old man stopped, and shouted at them in a loud voice:

'Mengde (Cao Cao's courtesy title). Isn't that Mengde on the horse?'

Cao Cao was so startled that the color drained from his face. He urged Chen Gong forward.

'Lü is my family name. Your father stayed in my home last night, but left hurriedly this morning. He never imagined that you would come.'

Chen Gong thought that running into any old acquaintances at this stage could only bode evil. But he could not convince Cao Cao, and they followed the old man into the manor.

Cao Cao and Chen Gong sat facing each other in the manor hall.

Their host was very hospitable. He sat them down and ordered his servants to prepare food and wine. Lü Boshe then personally took a blue and white patterned wine jug to the

自己抱着一个蓝地白花酒樽到前村去沽酒。陈宫心细，悄声地问曹操这老汉的来路，曹操哈哈笑道：

"不妨事，吕伯奢是我父的八拜之交，两家一直来往不断的。在这里就和自己家里一样。"曹操说着叹了口气，"只是家父逃离家园，不知道投奔何处去了。"

两人不说话。他们都想，吕伯奢上了年纪，走起来慢吞吞的，前村总得有三五里吧。曹操抬头望望天色，一个小僮笑嘻嘻地端了一盏灯进来放在桌上，望着曹操只是笑，笑得他心烦。他用手扶了一下头上蓝色宽边的风帽，两眼侧边的鱼尾纹显得更深了。

厨房里的人喊小僮的名字，他听了扭转身跑去，露出腰里拖着两根长长的粗麻绳，飘飘的。曹操看了不响。

赶了半夜一天的路，最好是有张铺倒头就睡。可是不行，只能坐着，你看我，我看你。

曹操想赶去瞌睡，只好起来踱步，踱到窗口，看院子里的景致。小小的院子里还养着花，旁边是一大间厨房，通后院，从那里传来猪吃食的哼声，想是厕所，看了半日又回来坐下。

next village to buy wine. A cautious Chen Gong quietly interrogated Cao Cao about the old man's background.

Cao Cao smiled: 'Don't worry. Lü Boshe was my father's sworn brother and our two families have been close for years. Being here is the same as being at home.' Then he sighed, 'It's just that my father has fled from home, and goodness knows where he has gone for shelter!'

The two men fell silent. They were both thinking of Lü Boshe, an aged man, walking slowly to the next village which must be four or five *li* away. Cao Cao raised his head and looked at the darkening sky. A young servant, smiling broadly, carried a lamp into the room and set it down on the table. Still smiling, he gazed at Cao Cao until Cao Cao became irritated by the smile. Cao Cao stretched out a hand to touch the wide-brimmed blue hat he wore. The fish-tail creases at the corner of his eyes seemed deeper than ever.

From the kitchen someone called the young servant's name and he immediately turned and ran off, two long, coarse hemp ropes tied around his waist swinging behind him. Cao Cao watched him silently.

After a day and a half of steady travel, what they wanted most was to unroll their bedding and sleep, but this was impossible; they could only sit there and do nothing.

Cao Cao, longing to doze off, strolled over to the window for a look at the view of the courtyards. The tiny courtyard contained a flower bed, and next to it he could see a huge kitchen connecting it with the back courtyard. From the courtyard he could hear the sound of pigs feeding - or was this an outhouse? He gazed for a long time and then returned to his seat.

睡意没有了。曹操竖起了耳朵，眼睛看着陈宫。

"听，这是什么？"

"磨刀。"

是磨刀，陈宫说得不错。磨刀干什么？曹操忽然想。问题是简单的，但可以有种种不同回答。在曹操的头脑里一下子忽地触发了一连串疑问，像花筒放到一半出现了海市蜃楼的灯彩似的，一个连着一个。曹操不由得摸了一下解下放在桌上的刀。那个小僮为什么冲着我笑？他屁股后面吊着的麻绳是做什么的？这个老头子为什么不派小僮去沽酒，偏要自己去？难道小僮连酒都打不来么？当然，有些事小孩子说不清楚，但不是打酒这样的小事。

曹操觉得自己的头发都竖起来了，鼻窝两边的纹路翕翕地动。

"你想干什么？"陈宫失声地问，他看见曹操从鞘里抽出了刀。

"我看看去！"

陈宫说不出话，眼睁睁看着他轻手轻脚一阵风似的掩门出去。

过了一会曹操回来时，眼睛都红了，却又嘻嘻地笑。

"我杀、杀了他们的人。他们家再没有人了，都杀光了。从厨房杀到后院、上房，见一个杀一个，杀到猪圈，才看见

Suddenly his drowsiness left him. He pricked up his ears and looked at Chen Gong.

'Listen! What's that?'

'It sounds like a knife being sharpened.'

Chen Gong was right. But why? This one question could have many explanations. The thought triggered off a whole string of questions in Cao Cao's mind like the sparks emitted by the fuse of a fire cracker. Cao Cao instinctively stroked the knife he had unbuckled from his waist and placed on the table. Why had the servant boy smiled at me like that? Why was that rope hanging from his waist? Why didn't the old man send him to buy the wine, but insist on going himself? It was not possible that the boy could not manage to fetch a jug of wine. Some things can't be explained to a child; but a simple thing like fetching wine?

Cao Cao felt his hair stand on end, and his nostrils quivered.

'What are you going to do?' Chen Gong said, when he noticed Cao Cao unsheathe his knife.

'I'm going to take a look around!'

Chen Gong, unable to utter a sound, watched with his eyes wide open as Cao Cao quietly slipped out of the door like a puff of wind.

A short while later Cao Cao returned, eyes reddened, but laughing to himself.

'I've killed them, killed all of them, every single member of their family. I slew everyone one by one from the kitchen to the backyard to the main hall. Only when I reached the pigsty did I see they had used the rope to truss the pig to the

他们已经用麻绳把猪绑在架子上……"曹操嘻嘻地笑,好像连陈宫也不认识了。

陈宫一句话也说不出来。陈宫两天前才认识曹操,立即为他的亢爽的风度、豪迈的言语打动了。这是一位少年英雄,有非凡的抱负和胆略,这才决心把自己后半世的命运交付给他,弃了官一起亡命。他不知道曹操是个宁愿错到底也不回头的人。

曹操好像换了一个人,陈宫想。在中牟县大堂上称自己为"府君",路上当他是朋友,目前就像奴仆似的呼来喝去了。曹操显得越发镇静了,声音低而坚定,他不管陈宫的抗议,只命令说,"收拾收拾,把马拉出来,到厨房里拉些稻草放在院子四角,找火种来……"

当他们跨上马背,离开庄院时,火势已经沸沸扬扬地了,西北风大,顷刻一片通红。

他们在前面路口又遇上了该死的沽酒回来的吕伯奢。还未等他清醒过来,曹操只一刀,他就倒在路旁。

"还是让他一起去了痛快!"曹操向瞪大了眼睛说不出话的陈宫平静地说,"他回去看了他的家,会发疯,会到亭长那里去报告的,这条老狗!"曹操清了一下嗓子,"老子

rafters ...' Cao Cao beamed, and barely seemed aware of Chen Gong's presence.

Chen Gong was struck dumb. He had only met Cao Cao two days before, but he had immediately been impressed by his haughty, straightforwaed manner and bold speech. This was a heroic youth with uncommon ambitions, courage and resourcefulness. These qualities had convinced him to place his life in Cao Cao's hands, abandon his post and accompany him in flight. He had not known that Cao Cao was a man who would rather commit innumerable errors than change his ways.

To Chen Gong, Cao Cao had suddenly become a different man. In Zhongmou County, Cao Cao had addressed him as 'Your Honor', and on the road had treated him as a friend. But now he was ordering him about like a servant. Cao Cao became even calmer, and ignoring Chen Gong's protests, firmly ordered him to clean up the place, lead the horses from the stables, take kindling straw from the kitchen and spread it in the courtyard, and then find some live cinders ...

As they mounted their horses and left the manor, the fire was burning fiercely, thanks to a strong northwest wind which had whipped it to a brilliant blaze in minutes.

At the first intersection, they encountered the ill-fated Lü Boshe returning from the next village. Before he knew it he had fallen at the roadside with a stroke from Cao Cao's blade.

'It's best to let him go with the rest,' Cao Cao told his speechless, wide-eyed companion. 'If he went back home, he'd go crazy; he'd report it to the village constable, the filthy dog!' Cao Cao cleared his throat. 'I still have many things to do. I

还有大事业要干，不能心软误了大事，错就错到底！账要等将来一总算。懂吗？"说罢，曹操在马屁股上甩了一鞭，向前驰去了。

他们来到了一家旅店。

曹操没事人似的吩咐店家给马上足草料，要了五斤酒、两盆肉，就大吃起来。陈宫只在一边看。曹操没有话，他知道陈宫想说些什么，觉得都没有回答的必要，因为一切都早对他解释清楚了。吃完了肉，酒还剩下一半。曹操解下腰刀，脱下上衣卷成一卷，枕着，立即倒在炕上睡着了。

第二天天亮，麻雀在窗前檐下吵成了一片。曹操醒来，眼睛在屋里四下搜寻，什么都不见。一个鲤鱼打挺，曹操翻下炕来。曹操看见桌上放着一封信，用刀压着，刀是从他的衣服卷里抽出来的。

曹操打开信，慢慢地读了，脸上漾出了恶意的笑。"没用的东西！"曹操喊，被自己的声音吓了一跳。

can't let a soft heart get in the way of important affairs. If I'm wrong, I'll be wrong right to the finish! We'll settle the final account later. Understand?' Cao Cao finished speaking and whippecd his horse's rump, urging it forward.

They arrived at an inn.

Cao Cao told the innkeeper to give the horses plenty of fodder, then ordered five jugs of wine, two plates of meat, and tucked into a large meal. Chen Gong watched silently from the side. Cao Cao didn't speak. He knew what Chen Gong had to say, and felt no need to reply - he'd already explained everything to him earlier on. After finishing his meat and downing half the wine, Cao Cao unbuckled his knife, stripped off his coat, rolled it into a pillow, and lay down on it and fell asleep.

At dawn the next morning he awoke to the sound of sparrows twittering noisily under the eaves outside his window. Opening his eyes, he gazed around the room. Everything was gone. Jerking himself into a standing position, Cao Cao leapt off the bed and saw a letter on the table weighted down with his own knife.

Cao Cao opened the letter and read slowly, a malicious smile spreading across his face. 'Useless fool!' he bellowed. The sound of his voice was so loud that he even terrified himself.

长坂坡

本剧讲述东汉末年中国三国鼎立之时刘备和曹操之间的故事。三个敌对国之间的争斗持续了约半个世纪（220—280）。在京剧和其他中国传统剧种中都有不少关于"三国"的戏。本剧的主角是英勇善战的赵云和刘备的夫人。

——编者

曹操选了个小山坡纵马上去，身后跟着一大批随从。

曹操从容地在山坡上走了一转。眼前一片桑林，更前面就是一大片开阔地，左面是一条浅浅的小河，河背后又是一座小山。他觉得这地方选得很好，很隐蔽。从下面望上来只能看见那片桑林。可是从坡上下望，战场上的动静却能看得清清楚楚。

曹操脸上漾着微笑。这笑是难得的，轻易不会在他脸上出现。这说明，他目前的心境是平静的、愉快的，他尽力控制着不笑出声来，可是到底还是漾出了微笑。自从战斗打响

The Long Slope

This opera recounts the story of the conflict which took place between Liu Bei and Cao Cao during the Eastern Han dynasty when China was split into three warring factions. These factions later developed into three antagonistic countries which existed in a state of confrontation for approximately half a century (220-280). Various versions of the story occur in the repertoire of the Beijing Opera and other forms of Chinese traditional opera. The protagonists in this opera are the valiant general Zhao Yun and the wife of Liu Bei.

-Ed.-

Followed by a large retinue, Cao Cao galloped up the slope of a small hill he had chosen as a lookout.

He rode leisurely around its peak, examining the terrain on every side: beneath him was a mulberry forest and further on an open plain; to the east was a small river, beyond which rose another hill. He was satisfied that he had closen a well-sheltered spot, for an observer looking upwards from below could only see the mulberries; while from the top all movements on the battlefield were visible.

There was a slight smile on Cao Cao's face. As he was not a man who habitually smiled, this was a rare moment for him; though he did his best to conceal his feelings, the smile appeared nevertheless. He had good reason to be pleased, for

以后，一切似乎都按着他事先的安排发展，刘备的小股兵力看来是必然的要消灭了。现在他只担心刘备逃得快，跑到远远的什么小地方躲起来，那就将依旧是一个隐患。可是出乎意料，刘备撤退得很慢，据情报说是给一大批难民拖住了。奇怪，他为什么不夹着尾巴快快溜掉呢？曹操想不出这理由。

眼前正是一片理想的战场。曹操打算把全部兵力都投放进去，进行一场彻底的歼灭战。身边的将军都派出去了，连负责保管他心爱的青虹宝剑的夏侯恩也不例外，只留下一个曹洪，随时向他汇报战场局势，并传布他的指示；此外就只有文职参谋人员，这中间有一直不声不响保持着沉默的徐庶。

曹操很懂得人才的重要，在多年的政治军事斗争中逐步领悟了这是使自己的事业得以成功必不可少的重要条件，同时也积累了许多经验了。他需要武将也需要谋士，懂得和不同对手打交道时需要使用不同的方法。今天他特地把徐庶放在身边，亲热地说这说那，就是想让徐庶在战场上亲眼看到刘备的队伍的惨败与覆灭。也许在事实的教育下这个和刘备关系密切、一直闷声不响的谋士会有所转变。……

since the battle had begun everything seemed to have proceeded according to plan. Liu Bei's small force was sure to be wiped out. His only worry now was that Liu Bei might flee too fast and escape to some faraway place where he could hide and remain a potential threat. But quite surprisingly Liu Bei's withdrawal was very slow; according to reports from the field, his movements had been hampered by a flood of refugees. It puzzled Cao Cao that he had not run off by himself.

With such an ideal battleground before him, Cao Cao intended to use all his forces to destroy the enemy completely. All his generals had been sent into battle, even Xiahou En, the custodian of his prized Green Rainbow Sword. Only Cao Hong, his cousin, remained behind to act as a messenger to transmit his orders and report occasionally on the progress of the battle. The others were nonmilitary personnel, his advisers and counselors, among whom was one who had remained silent throughout - Xu Shu.

Cao Cao was a man who valued talent. In the course of many years of pilitical and military struggle, he had firmly grasped the truth that men of ability were important if not indispensable to the success of his cause. His experience told him that he needed good counselors no less than good fighters, and that different tactics must be used in dealing with different people. Today he had purposely kept Xu Shu at his side and conversed with him kindly, for he wanted him to witness with his own eyes Liu Bei's disastrous defeat and annihilation. This silent but exceedingly clever man, up to now a close friend of Liu Bei's, might be persuaded by the grim realities to change his allegiance ...

"元直先生，这真是一片好战场。弄得好，天黑以前战斗就能结束了。"曹操眯起了眼，像是自言自语地打量着山角。

徐庶嘴角似乎也动了一下，却听不见声音，也许那回答恰好被一阵紧密的鼓声与鼓噪压下了。

这鼓声，还有伴随而来的喊杀声使曹操耸起了耳朵。声音是从山角那面传来的，奇怪的是这并非两军厮杀中的混乱喊声，听来全是从自己部队中发出的，由远而近，像一阵阵潮水似的传来。紧跟着，一匹白马上的一片白色影子从山角出现了，夹杂着一股闪闪的耀眼银光，那是马上将军手中挥舞的宝剑带来的。

也许这敌将是被有意地诱引过来的吧。把对手引到眼前的旷地中，再加以包围、歼灭。曹操微微地颔首。紧跟着白马后面果然出现了骑着黑马穿着黑色战袍的许褚和张郃，他们跟在白马后面，紧紧地咬着。白马突然在小河前停下，马头被掉转过来。张郃也吃惊地煞住了马。他们在马上彼此打量了一下，真的只是一刹那，只见白光起处，张郃用枪挡了一下，那白马又从山角处飞驰而去了。

曹操不高兴地哼了一下鼻子，因为跟前出现的局面和他的预计不相符。怎能让一员敌将如此自由地进出于自己的队

'Mr. Yuanzhi (Xu Shu's courtesy title), this is indeed a good battle field. If everything goes well, the battle will be over before nightfall,' remarked Cao Cao, scanning the foot of the hill and talking to himself.

The corner of Xu Shu's mouth seemed to twitch slightly, but no sound emerged. Perhaps his reply had been smothered by a sudden roll of drums.

Cao Cao pricked up his ears at the sound of the drums and the shouts that followed. They seemed to come from around a curve in the hill. Strange to say, there was none of the din and whoop of two armies clashing. The sounds all seemed to come from his own troops and were approaching steadily like a tide. The next minute a solitary white figure on a white horse rounded the curve, brandishing a sword that continually emitted flashes of silvery light.

Cao Cao recognized this as an enemy general and nodded slightly. It must be that he was being lured to this open place to be ambushed and killed. Sure enough, following the white horse were two of his own generals, Xu Chu and Zhang He, in black battle dress and on black steeds. They were pursuing the white horse closely. At the edge of the river the white knight suddenly reined in and turned his horse around. Surprised by this move, Zhang He also checked his horse. The two eyed each other for a few seconds, then a flash of white light rose and Zhang He raised his lance to ward off the blow. In an instant, the white horse had sped past him and disappeared again around the curve.

Up on the hill Cao Cao snorted in disgust. Things had not gone according to plan. How was it that an enemy general

伍中呢？张郃、许褚的惊慌失措、无力阻止更使他不舒服。这一切都是不能容忍的。他微侧了头，随侍在身边的曹洪立即小心地凑了过来。

"去看看这都是怎么一回事？"

徐庶是认出了那马上的白色影子的，可是也弄不清他为什么突然出现在大军密集的曹军核心地区，而且只一瞬就又不见了。

"那就是常山的赵子龙，赵四将军。一员虎将。"徐庶说。

不必说曹操与徐庶，就是刘备阵营中人也不能理解赵云这种近于儿戏的无意识的冒险行径。刘备集团被曹军冲得七零八落以后分头逃散了，连刘备的两位夫人在内；这时只有赵云还在身边。他接受了一个艰难的任务，去寻找和护送失散了的两位主母和在襁褓中的王位继承人——阿斗出险。这就是赵云拨转马头重新杀进曹营的真实原因，连张飞看了也莫名奇妙，他想赵云不是发了疯就是投降曹操去了。

赵云也真的好像发了疯。一匹白马，一条银枪，杀进了黑压压一片的曹营。他冲过了山角，看见面前是一片宽广的平地，不像有被冲散的自己人队伍，就立即拨转马头走出去，实在无心与张郃他们交手。

could come and go so freely among his troops? And why were both Xu Chu and Zhang He panic-stricken and powerless to stop him? Cao Cao turned his head slightly and at this bidding Cao Hong edged up to him.

'Go and see what this is all about,' he commanded.

Xu Shu had recognized the white knight, but he was also perplexed as to why he had appeared so suddenly among Cao Cao's troops and just as suddenly disappeared again.

'That was Zhao Zilong (Zhao Yun) of Changshan, Zhao the Fourth General,' he said, 'a tiger of a warrior.'

Not even the people in Liu Bei's camp, let alone Cao Cao and Xu Shu, could guess the reason for Zhao Yun's taking this seemingly motiveless risk that was more like a child's game. Liu Bei's followers had been scattered and each was fleeing on his own. His two wives and infant son, Ah Dou, were lost, too. Only Zhao Yan was at his side and this faithful general now took upon himself the task of finding and escorting back the two ladies and Liu Bei's heir. So instead of following the retreat, he had turned around and charged into the ranks of the enemy. Even the formidable Zhang Fei (Liu Bei's sworn brother) was astounded at this. Zhao Yun must be mad, or perhaps he was giving himself up to Cao Cao.

Zhao Yun's actions seemed mad. Alone and armed with a single lance, he had fought his way into the thick of Cao Cao's army that numbered close to 100,000 men. When he rounded the curve, he saw before him an open plain on which there were no signs of stragglers or fleeing troops, and since he was in no mood to fight Zhang He and the others, he turned around and galloped off in another direction.

　　被曹洪带了来向曹操汇报的张郃也说不出更有说服力的判断，只是恨恨地赌咒，"让我再把他引过来，让埋伏在桑林里的箭手把他射成一只刺猬，这个该死的！"张郃斜着眼看着曹操身边的徐庶。

　　曹操铁青着脸不说话。张郃胯下的战马焦躁不安地移换着前蹄。徐庶轻轻的像是只想使自己听见似的说，"这可是一员难得的战将啊！"

　　这时，骑着白马的将军的身影又从山角处出现了。这次赵云是想杀出重围。记起这里曾有过一片开阔地，突围也许容易些，这才重寻旧路摸了回来。他这时已经完成了使命，他无意中在一处居民墙角找到了身受重伤的糜夫人，并从她手中接过了阿斗，解开战袍，揣在怀里。就在这时，糜夫人跳进了身边的一口枯井。赵云有点吃惊，也有点伤感，可是他的心是平静的。他明白自己已经在极端的困难中完成了使命。他明白，一个女人和她的独子的价值应该怎样衡量，对女人来说，重要的是保住自己的贞操，特别是眼前的乱军之中。她

Zhang He was brought before Cao Cao to give a report. He could offer no plausible reason for Zhao Yun's conduct and only cursed, 'That damned fellow! Let me lure him to this place again and we'll have the archers hidden among the mulberry trees shoot at him until he looks like a hedgehog.' As he spoke, he cast a glance sideways at Xu Shu who was standing beside Cao Cao.

Cao Cao's face was a blank; he said nothing, But Zhang He's steed kept rapping its front hooves as if in agitation. Xu Shu now spoke, but whispered as if he did not want to be heard: 'This is, indeed, a great warrior; there's not one like him in a thousand!'

Meanwhile, the white knight on the white horse had reappeared around the curve. This time it was because he wanted to break through Cao Cao's encirclement and the open plain seemed a likely place. He had completed more than half his mission, when he had unexpectedly come upon Lady Mi, one of Liu Bei's two wives, sitting badly wounded beside the wall of a village house. She had handed him the infant Ah Dou and he had carefully placed the baby inside his breast plate next to his chest. As he did this, Lady Mi turned and leaped into a dry well. Though shocked and grieved, Zhao Yun was consoled by the fact that the most important part of his mission had been completed in spite of all the dangers and hardships. He knew, by feudal standards, what a woman and her only son were worth. For a woman, the most important thing was to preserve her chastity, especially in the present chaotic conditions of war. Now that the lady had found her peace at the bottom of a well, there was nothing more to worry

既已平安地睡在井里，就再也没有什么可担心了。而阿斗的价值则大不同，在这个小子身上寄托着姓刘的血统、皇位的正统……而这一切的价值，简直是难以估量的。

在山坡上的曹操一群人眼中,赵云也不再是那个旧赵云，他更勇敢、威武，更无顾忌地杀过来了。紧紧围绕他身边的是一团逼眼的寒光，远远也能听见铁器撞击的响声，不只是人体，就是刀剑也阻挡不住他面前的路。在这位将军面前真的铺开了一条血路。

站在山坡上的曹操脸上结起的严霜渐渐融化了。只有他辨得出，赵云手里拿着的正是他心爱的青虹剑，这是"削铁如泥"的名剑。他明白这剑是怎样到了赵云手里的。剑是宝贵的，但更要紧的是使用宝剑的人。在饭桶手里，名剑也没有什么用处，甚至保不住自己的脑袋。在曹操心底，强烈地萌发了奇特的贪欲，抑制不住。他看了一下身边，看看张邰，又看看阻挡不住赵云纷纷倒下来的将军、兵士。他一个字一个字地向曹洪口授了军令：

"赵云所到之处，不许暗放冷箭。只要活赵云，不要死子龙。违令者斩！"

赵云觉得奇怪，只顾杀得快意，却不遇见一弓一矢。张邰也觉得奇怪,丞相何以要花这样沉重的代价活捉一个赵云。他不懂得，曹操对一只刺猬实在并无兴趣。

about. But the infant Ah Dou was another case. This baby was the scion of the imperial Liu family, the legitmate heir to the throne of Han ... His life was of inestimable value.

In the eyes of Cao Cao and his followers on the hill, Zhao Yun was a different man now, more daring, more powerful and more reckless than ever before. Cold steel besieged him on all sides; clashes of iron resounded in the distance, but neither man nor metal could stop him. The white knight was literally fighting his way over a path of blood.

The frost on Cao Cao's face melted. He alone recognized the weapon in Zhao Yun's hand: it was his own Green Rainbow Sword, a weapon that could 'slash through iron like clay', and he knew well how it had come into Zhao Yun's possession. The sword was precious, but more precious was the man who now wielded it. The best sword in the world was useless in the hands of a good-for-nothing who could not even defend his own head. An inordinate and irrepressible desire to win over this gallant white knight burned fiercely in Cao Cao's breast. He looked around at his followers, at Zhang He, and at his soldiers and generals who in trying to stop Zhao Yun were being cut down one after the other. Turning to Gao Hong, he issued his orders:

'Zhao Yun must not be sniped at. He must be captured alive. Anyone disobeying these orders shall be executed.'

Meanwhile, Zhao Yun found it strange that while he had fought so hard and so well, he had not been struck by a single arrow. Zhang He, too, wondered why the Prime Minister should be willing to pay such a high price for the capture of Zhao Yun. He did not know that Cao Cao had no interest in a 'hedgehog'.

　　丞相的将令下达以后，只见一批批队伍向赵云身边包围过去，没有人敢放箭，连交手时都小心着。最好是他自己跌下马来，捉住，缚起。可是无效，赵云还是笔直地一路杀过去了。

　　赵云杀得性起，一路杀到小河边。遥遥望见远处疏林中露出了张飞部队的黑旗，望见张飞命令兵士在马尾缚了树枝来回奔跑引起的阵阵尘雾。赵云摆脱了连续不断涌上来的敌兵，向斜刺里驰去，又突然折回，在上游一座桥头终于发现了横枪立马的张飞。

　　赵云终于在二里外的另一座树林深处找到了刘备他们一伙，正垂头丧气地坐在地上休息。赵云高兴了，但刘备却淡淡的说：

　　"你一个人回来了。"

　　赵云这时才忽地记起了藏在怀中的阿斗，背过身去，轻轻解开了铠甲、内衣。阿斗正睡得香甜，胖胖的小脸偎依着赵云汗透了的前胸。

　　赵云抱了阿斗，猛地转身，双手捧上去，没有话，满脸惊喜的笑。刘备简直呆住了，好半日，不知说什么才好。

When the Prime Minister's orders were announced, his troops began closing in upon the lone white knight from all sides, but none dared let fly an arrow. Even those who engaged him in combat had to be careful about their blows. If only he could be thrown off his horse, seized and bound! But that did not happen, and Zhao Yun pressed ahead.

Zhao Yun fought bravely until he had driven them to the side of a brook. From afar he saw Zhang Fei's black banners through the trees and the dust storm created by the tree branches tied to the tails of the horses ridden by Zhang Fei's men. Zhao Yun slipped away from the soldiers swarming about him and charged down a trail which led away from the main road. He then turned back abruptly and from a bridgehead saw Zhang Fei riding his horse with his long spear in hand.

Before long, Zhao Yun came upon Liu Bei and his party in the depths of another forest about a mile from the bridgehead. Dejected, they were resting on the ground. Zhao Yun was glad to see his master and quickly dismounted from his horse. Liu Bei asked him:

"You returned all by yourself?"

Suddenly Zhao Yun remembered that Ah Dou was concealed in his breast. Zhao Yun turned around and carefully removed his armor and inner garments. Ah Dou was peacefully asleep there, his plump little face snuggled up in Zhao Yun'a sweating breast.

With Ah Dou cradled in his arms, Zhao Yun quickly turned around, and without a word presented the child to Liu Bei. Liu Bei was stunned and for a long while didn't know what to say.

龙凤呈祥

东汉末年，大规模农民起义之后，中国形成了由曹操、刘备、孙权领导的三个政治集团。曹操死后，三个政治集团的领导相继称帝，形成三国鼎立的局面，达半个世纪之久。

《三国演义》是流传极广的中国古典名著之一，其中记叙了刘备和孙权如何联合对抗曹操的故事。小说描写刘备系正宗皇室后裔，一位正人君子。

京剧经常上演由这部分内容改编的戏《龙凤呈祥》。剧中乔玄劝说吴国太相中刘备为婿的念白和唱段最为有名。因该剧生、旦、净、丑行当齐全，故多年来一直久演不衰。

——编者

刘皇叔坐在长江船上，心里只是闷闷的，也无心细看两岸风景。这些时他是很有点埋怨起诸葛亮来了。自从三顾茅

The Dragon and the Phoenix Show Their Colors

In the late Han dynasty, after a large-scale peasant uprising, political power in China gradually became divided between three factions headed by Cao Cao, Liu Bei, and Sun Quan respectively. After Cao Cao's death, these three factions became the basis of the Three Kingdoms, which governed China for half a century.

The highly influential ancient Chinese novel The Romance of the Three Kingdoms chronicles how the factions headed by Liu Bei and Sun Quan united against Cao Cao in a power struggle. This novel depicts Liu Bei as being both the true descendant of rhe royal familly as well as a model statesman.

Among its most outstanding features of this frequently performed Beijing Opera is the lengthy aria in which Qiao Xuan urges the Empress Dowager of the Kingdom of Wu to take Liu Bei as her son-in-law. One of the reasons this opera's popularity has remained undiminished for so many years is that it includes the full range of Chinese operatic roles: 'sheng', 'dan', 'jing', and 'chou'.

-Ed.-

Liu Bei sat perturbed on a boat floating down the Yangtze River, paying no attention to the fine scenery along the way. He was upset about the famous statesman and strategist

庐，把这位"卧龙先生"请出了山，许久以来，仗着他的出
谋划策，使自己身边的一支小小队伍冲过了重重险阻，逐步
坚实壮大起来。事实证明他确是一位信得过的参谋策划人才，
只是不免有些自作主张，遇事也不大和自己商议。就像这回，
一口应允了孙吴的亲事，让自己轻车简从过江招赘，就全是
诸葛亮一手包揽说定的。尽管自己多么不情愿，到底还是被
他送上船，出发了。这一去是吉是凶，心里简直一些都没有
底，临别时诸葛只是笑着说，"不要紧，只管前去，一切都包
在亮的身上。"可是他的葫芦里到底卖的什么药，却只有天知
道。刘备这时觉得自己已经不再是什么皇叔、国主，却成了
诸葛手中玩弄的一只筹码……这样想着时就越发不舒服起来。

　　刘备回头看看，全副武装的四弟赵云正警惕地站在自己
身旁，心里总算多少添了一些安全感。这是一位忠心耿耿，勇
敢的将军，就是在千军万马之中，也能自由进出，如入无人
之境的。不过，这次深入一个不可知的充满了敌意的国度，即
使是赵子龙，万一碰上麻烦，也能保着自己杀出重围么？

　　刘备忽地想起，临行之前，诸葛曾神秘地和赵云在一起

Zhuge Liang. He had made three visits to Zhuge Liang's thatched hut finally succeeding in persuading this 'Sleeping Dragon' to give up his temporary retirement from the political arena. Ever since, Liu Bei had relied on Zhuge Liang's strategies and schemes, and as a result Liu Bei's troops survived numerous difficulties, and grew in strength. Zhuge Liang had proven himself to be a trustworthy person of extraordinary ability as a strategist. His faults were that he often decided things on his own in an arbitrary way, and seemed reluctant to confer with Liu Bei. For instance, Liu Bei's traveling down the river to marry into the Sun family of the Kingdom of Wu was all arranged by Zhuge Liang. Although Liu Bei was not entirely willing to enter into this marriage, the boat was already heading for Wu. Liu Bei had not the slightest idea whether his adventure would turn out to be a success or a disaster. When he saw Liu Bei off, Zhuge Liang had smiled and said, 'Take it easy. I'll take care of the rest.' But what did he have up his sleeve? Liu Bei no longer felt he was the emperor's uncle, but simply a card in Zhuge Liang's hand ... He was becoming more upset each moment.

Liu Bei felt a greater sense of security when he realized that his brother-in-arms, Zhao Yun, was standing beside him, dressed in full armor. Zhao Yun was a brave and loyal general who could hold his own in a battle of ten thousand. But this time they were going to an enemy state. Who could guarantee that Zhao Yun could bring him out alive if the going got rough?

Liu Bei recalled that before leaving home. Zhuge Liang had conferred privately with Zhao Yun; but it was rash for him to

谈了好一会子话，也许他心里有底也说不定，可又不便低声下气地打听，只好装作镇定，冷冷地说：

"四弟，这回来到东吴招亲，非比寻常，遇事可要多加小心。"

"主公不必担忧，先生临行时已给了赵云三道锦囊妙计了。"

刘备从赵云的口气中听出了诸葛在将士中间的威信。他从赵云手中接过藏在贴身里衣中的锦囊时，心里不禁在想，也许自己不该对这位军师先生产生任何疑虑。

锦囊打开以后，里面藏着一张写了玄妙诗句的纸片，有点像神签，刘备不禁又微微皱起了双眉。好在下面还有两句比较着实的话，"君臣来到东吴地，须到相府谒乔玄"。这时，刘备脸上又漾出了淡淡的微笑。

乔玄，这倒是一个关键性的人物，是一个可以也应该打开的缺口。吴国的当权者，国主孙权和都督周瑜，还有下面的将佐、士卒，好像都对占了荆州不还的自己充满了敌意与义愤，只有这个乔玄，看来似乎还像一个中间派。

赵云是不知道乔玄的底细的，刘备简单地说给他听了。

make any inquires at this point, so he feigned calm, and said casually,

'Brother Zhao, this trip to the Kingdom of Wu to marry into the Sun family is a rather uncommon one, so we must be more careful.'

'Don't worry, master. Zhuge Liang has given me an embroidered pouch containing three ingenious plots.'

From Zhao Yun's expression, Liu Bei could sense the prestige Zhuge Liang enjoyed among the generals and soldiers. When Zhao Yun gave him the embroidered pouch, he began to feel that maybe it was unnecessary to have any suspicion about this military counselor.

From the embroidered purse he removed a piece of paper on which many abstruse poems were written. Liu Bei frowned when he realized these poems resembled the inscriptions used by fortune tellers. As he read on, he discovered two sentences which seemed more palpable than the rest: 'When the two of you arrive at the Kingdom of Wu, you should call on Qiao Xuan.' Liu Bei's frown turned into a smile.

Qiao Xuan was actually a key figure who could provide solutions to critical problems. The two men who held the actual power in the Kingdom if Wu were Sun Quan and Zhou Yu, who along with their generals, commanders and soldiers, seemed to be hostile and indignant towards Liu Bei's occupation of Jingzhou. Qiao Xuan was the only person in power who was not committed in this fashion.

Zhao Yun knew little about Qiao Xuan, so Liu Bei introduced him briefly:

'Qiao Xuan has two daughters, both famous beauties. The

"乔玄有两个女儿，大乔、小乔，都是东吴有名的美人。大乔嫁给已经过世的孙权的哥哥孙策，小乔是周郎的夫人。所以乔国老是东吴的国丈啊！"接下去刘备吩咐赵云：

"等会下了船，安置好了，你就准备下一份厚礼，明天一早我们就去拜访。"

奉派前来迎接刘皇叔的是一文一武：吕范与贾华，他们都是孙吴国主孙权的贴身人。他们接刘备上了岸，放下了一颗心——鳌鱼到底上钩了。

乔玄，是吴国的太尉，政府的首脑。他是老一辈的重臣，和创业的孙坚、孙策父子关系密切，因为是姻亲，在当今的吴侯孙权母亲——国太面前，也是很有影响的人物。不过在孙权、周瑜等少壮当权派看来，则是老朽昏庸，已经成为前进道路上的绊脚石了。譬如孙权与周瑜定计，用许婚的方法把刘备骗来作为索回荆州的人质，事先就没有让乔玄知道。在战略上，乔玄，还有大夫鲁肃都是主张联刘拒曹的稳健派，这一直使孙权、周瑜很不满。碍手碍脚，影响他们不能放手执行自己的政策。只是因为他是老资格，一时也无可奈何。

乔玄今天朝罢归来，一路上看见悬灯结彩，街上行人也都显出非凡高兴的神色；自己府中，也有些异样，家里人都

older Qiao had married Sun Quan's older brother, Sun Ce, who was dead, and the younger was Zhou Yu's wife. Actually, Qiao Xuan is the father-in-law of the Kingdom of Wu!

After we arrive and get settled, prepare some generous gifts and we'll call Qiao Xuan."

A civil officer, Lü Fan, and a military officer, Jia Hua, were sent to receive Liu Bei. Both were close associates of Sun Quan. They felt relieved now. The turtle was on the hook at last.

Qiao Xuan was the military chief and the governor of the Kingdom of Wu. He was held in high esteem by the members of the older generation and had intimate relationships with the founders of the kingdom, Sun Jian and Sun Ce. Also through marriage, he had gained influence with Sun Quan's mother — Wu Guotai. But in the eyes of Sun Quan and Zhou Yu, Qiao Xuan was nothing more than a decrepit and fatuous old man, a stumbling block on their road to advancement. For instance, using marriage as a plot to take Liu Bei as a hostage in exchange for the return of the territory of Jingzhou was an idea developed by Sun Quan and Zhou Yu; Qiao Xuan knew nothing about it. In terms of military strategy, Qiao Xuan and Lu Su could be considered conservatives: they advocated uniting with Liu Bei to fight Cao Cao, the sovereign of the Kingdom of Wei. Sun Quan and Zhou Yu were rather displeased with this strategy. Qiao Xuan was a hindrance to their political goals. Yet because of his prestige, they could not do anything about him at this point.

On the way back from court, Qiao Xuan noticed that the street was decorated with lanterns and colored streamers and that the local people had extraordinarily cheerful expressions

在交头接耳地议论着什么。心里纳闷，把老家人乔福叫来一问，才听说了那个通国皆知惟独自己被蒙在鼓里的大新闻。这是不能不使他生气的。正在这时，门上通报，刘皇叔前来拜会。

刘备带领赵云来到乔府进行了一次短暂的礼仪性的拜访。留下了一份厚礼。乔玄送走了刘备，心里盘算，应该立即进宫给国太道喜，顺便探一下口风。这样一桩非比寻常的政治婚姻，自己竟完全不得与闻，实在可气。至于孙、刘两家结成婚媾的本身，在他看来倒是一件大好事。对抗曹操的联合阵线，这样一来就将更加牢靠，只是孙权、周瑜他们未必肯。这中间难道真的有什么花样么？

使乔玄吃惊的是，被蒙在鼓里的不只是他这个太尉，就连孙权和郡主尚香的母亲也丝毫没有听到任何消息。乔玄知道自己的机会来了，"这样大事，太后不知，谁敢作主？"问得好。

"是啊，这是哪个的主意呀？"

"莫非是二千岁的主意？"乔玄的话说得顺理成章，听不出这中间带着某种意气。

于是吴侯、二千岁孙权被召进宫来了。

孙权是个魁梧壮实的汉子，紫棠色的面颊下端长着密麻麻的一把漂亮发红的胡子，因此老百姓背后都叫他"紫髯

on their faces. There was also something unusual taking place at his own house: the members of his family were going around whispering things to each other. When he questioned his old servant Qiao Fu and learned he was the only one still in the dark, he became angry. But at that very mement, it was announced that Liu Bei had arrived.

The visit was formal and brief. Liu Bei presented a generous gift to the Qiao family. After seeing Liu Bei off, Qiao Xuan decided to go to the palace to visit the King's mother, Wu Guotai, and sound her out. That he had not been informed of such an unusual political marriage made him both furious and suspicious that something tricky was involved. From his point of view, the marriage of the Sun and Liu families was in fact a good thing, for it would align previously hostile forces against Cao Cao; though there was a possibity that Sun Quan and Zhou Yu would fail to give their approval. There was something fishy about the whole business!

Qiao Xuan was surprised to discover that he was not alone in his ignorance of the marriage. When he learned that even Sun Quan's mother, Wu Guotai, did not know about it, Qiao Xuan said to her, 'Since even Your Ladyship knew nothing about this great affair, who could have made the arrangement?'

'That's right, who's idea was it?'

'Perhaps we should consult our sovereign ...' Qiao Xuan's suggestion was entirely reasonable and seemed to embody no personal feelings.

Sun Quan was then summoned to the court.

Sun Quan was a tall, well-built man with ruddy cheeks and a beautiful bushy moustache which inspired people to

儿"，这是带有某种亲昵意味的。他继承了父兄的余荫，团结了一批年轻将领，是个很有些雄心壮志的地方割据者，但对母亲却是恭顺畏惧的。他明白，站在母亲后面的有一群像乔玄那样的老家伙，不能不认真对待。

孙权在母亲身边坐了，觑见乔玄先已进宫，心里更是老大不舒服。国太劈头就问，"孙、刘二家结亲，可是儿的主意？"孙权一下子手足无措了，白了乔玄一眼，吞吞吐吐地回答，"这……儿臣不知。""嗯！"吴国太拉下了脸，孙权这时再也沉不住气，只好如实交代。

吴国太对孙权、周瑜共同策划的计谋发了大怒："那刘备既然久借荆州不还，儿就该发兵遣将，与他争斗，夺回荆州。怎么，你将胞妹做成美人之计，纵然得了荆州，岂不被天下耻笑！"

乔玄这时也站出来帮腔。孙权就顺手指出他的女婿其实倒正是主谋，堵他的嘴。

"怎么，又是那周郎！他这明明是要害你呀！"

"多口！"对乔玄，孙权就是这样的不客气，不过对母亲

call him 'Purple Beard' behind his back. He carried on his father's and brother's careers and gathered around himself a group of young generals. He was a local ruler of lofty aspirations and great ideals. Nevertheless, he was both respectful of and submissive to his mother. He understood that the people who stood behind his mother were a bunch of old-timers like Qiao Xuan who had to be dealt with delicately.

Sun Quan sat down next to his mother and felt a twinge of disappointment when he discovered that Qiao Xuan was already there. Wu Guotai asked him directly: 'Is the marriage between the Sun and Liu families your idea?' Sun Quan became flustered and glanced hostilely at Qiao Xuan. When he replied 'Well, I ... I don't have any idea,' Wu Guotai pulled a long face to evince her displeasure. Sun Quan now realized he could hide the facts no longer and made a clean breast of the whole story.

Wu Guotai's criticism of Suan Quan and Zhou Yu's plan was hard to refute. She put it this way: 'Since Liu Bei refuses to return the long-occupied territory of Jingzhou, you should have deployed troops to fight him, and seize it back by force. But you've chosen to use your own sister as bait, so even if you regain Jingzhou, won't you be making a fool of yourself in front of everybody?'

Qiao Xuan stood up and added a few words of his own. And in order to silence Qiao Xuan, Sun Quan pointed out that it was Qiao Xuan's own son-in-law who was the chief plotter.

'Zhou Yu again! He obviously wants to get you in trouble!'

'Shut up!' Sun Quan could speak rudely to Qiao Xuan, but he had little choice but to pretend obedience to his mother.

的斥责却只能装出服服贴贴的样子，但背地里早已下定了决心：一定要杀掉刘备，这是不能让步的。

国太的发怒只是因为心爱的郡主竟被当作美人计的钓饵，大大伤害了自己的尊严。至于杀不杀刘备，那倒无关轻重。乔玄也看出了这一点，要紧的是，不能放弃机会，必须使国太对刘皇叔和他所代表的地方势力留下一个完整，美好的印象。

在孙权看来，乔玄这个糟老头儿恰似一个小丑、弄臣，在国太面前，竟用一个评话艺人的架势、声口，无耻地演说刘皇叔发光的家史和灿烂的战斗历程。他历数了刘备的先世是汉室中山靖王一派；使青龙刀的二弟关羽和用丈八矛的三弟张飞都是怎样英勇得了不得；四弟赵云在长坂坡前的战绩，和运筹帷幄的天才军师诸葛孔明。这些话孙权是不要听的，但国太却有兴趣，像听书似的为之神往了。不管孙权使过多少次眼色，表示了怎样的不耐，老头儿还是兴致勃勃地说下去，说下去。乔玄的结论是，这门亲事应该结的，是非结不可的。

孙权终于发作了，"不管怎么说刘备都配不上我的妹子！"

"配得的！"乔玄不肯让步。

吴国太制止了这场争论，决定第二天在甘露寺亲自面相刘备，再做定夺。

"国太若是相中了呢？"乔玄忙着追问。

In any case, the plot to kill Liu Bei had been hatched secretly, and he would make no compromise on that score.

Wu Guotai was furious about her beloved daughter being used as bait in a scheme of entrapment. This was a violation of the dignity of the Sun family. As for murdering Liu Bei, this was a matter to which she gave little attention. With this in mind, Qiao Xuan made sure to leave her with a favorable impression of Liu Bei and of his extensive authority in the State of Shu.

In the eyes of Sun Quan, Qiao Xuan was nothing more than a clown. But in front of Wu Guotai, he assumed the role of a storyteller and recounted Liu Bei's glorious family background and dazzling military accomplishments. He told her how Liu Bei's ancestors were members of the Han dynasty imperial family, and listed the heroic exploits of his famous brothers-in-arms: Guan Yu, with his Blue Dragon Sword; Zhang Fei, with his long spear; Zhao Yun with his military triumphs which took place at the Long Slope, and the brilliant strategist Zhuge Liang. Of course, Sun Quan hated listening to all that, but Wu Guotai was completely charmed. No matter how many times Sun Quan winked at Qiao Xuan to stop, the old fellow went on talking with great zest, ending up with a strong recommendation that the marriage knot should be tied.

Sun Quan erupted at last: 'In any case, Liu Bei isn't good enough for my sister!'

'He certainly is!' Qiao Xuan wouldn't give an inch either.

Wu Guotai put an end to the quarrel by deciding to meet Liu Bei the next day at the Temple of Sweet Dew.

'What if you do find him acceptable?' Qiao Xuan asked.

"招他作女婿。"

"母后若是相不上呢？"孙权紧接着问。

"那就由你处置。下去吧！"

孙权看来好像颇有把握，满意地匆匆走了。刘备的命运就要在明天决定，国太选婿的标准是什么，乔玄不能不加以考虑。

只有半天一夜的时间了，许多人都要为决定刘备、同时也是吴国的命运、前途抓紧做许多工作。

"刘备满脸花白胡子，哪里像个新郎？但愿母后看不中就好。"孙权越想越不舒服，"可是一旁插进个乔太尉却是讨厌的。天知道这老头子会说出什么'坏话'来。"当时天下群雄并起，各据一方，汉家天子只是曹操手中的一块招牌。尽管如此，姓刘的到底还有些未曾熄尽的余炎。在全国，在江东，还有着不小的威望。论出身，论门第，他们孙家哪里数得上。难保国太就不会产生招进一位阔女婿的兴趣。这都是值得警惕的。

出于同样的理由，乔玄担心的并不是刘皇叔的家世根基。只愁他那一脸胡子，配作郡主的新婚么？能通得过未来岳母的眼睛么？

孙权把吕范唤进宫来，商量对策。最后决定在甘露寺中，

'Then he'll become my son-in-law.'

'What if mother doesn't like him?' Sum Quan asked immediately.

'Then you'll take care of him. You may go now!'

Sun Quan felt confident about the outcome and left with satisfaction. Since Liu Bei's fate would be decided the next day, Qiao Xuan could not help worrying about the criteria she would use in making her decision.

In less than two days' time, many decisions had to be made concerning the fate of Liu Bei and the Kingdom of Wu.

'Liu Bei's hair is already graying: he hardly resembles a young groom. I can hardly imagine my honorable mother finding him acceptable.' The more Sun Quan thought about it, the more upset he became. What a nuisance it was that Qiao Xuan had hands in this business. Who could predict what sort of malicious remarks he would make. At present, a number of generals had established separatist regimes of their own, and the Han Emperor was but Cao Cao's pretence. However, if Liu poked and the ashes, there was a good chance of finding some burning embers and Liu's prestige had spread throughout the nation, particularly in the east. In terms of class origin and family status, the Sun family could not match the Liu family. Therefore, it was very likely that Wu Guotai would find it advantageous to have a rich son-in-law. All this made Sun Quan sharpen his vigilance.

What worried Qiao Xuan most of all was not Liu Bei's class origin but his gray beard, which might not pass his future mother-in-law's inspection.

Sun Quan summoned Lü Fan to the court to discuss counter

埋伏下一批刀手，由大将贾华统率，觑准时机，不问国太相亲得出怎样的结论，总之，刘备是非消灭不可的。

乔玄回府以后立即派人给刘备送去了"乌须药"，教给他使用的方法，这至少可以保证他瞒掉十岁年纪。此外，还提醒他要警惕席前有诈，保驾的将军最好是"内穿铠甲，外罩袍服"，准备对付意料之外其实是意料之中的事变。

甘露寺的大殿里摆下了筵席座位，换上了一色大红桌帏、椅帔。正中自然是太后的主位，两侧是未来"娇客"与相陪的主人席次。仪仗、执事人等穿梭地来往布置，安放酒果，排列桌椅。这时，在大殿两侧的回廊、厢房里，许多换了衣装的军士也正忙碌地将刀剑安置在身边的角落里。他们的统帅、东吴大将贾华，不时地探头探脑窥伺着殿前的动静。他是全副武装了的，腰间、背上插满了鞭、锏、锤、剑，手里还不住地搬弄着一把大刀。

就在这时，吴国太由乔玄陪同来到了佛殿，入了座。不久，刘备也到了。殿上奏起了细乐，乔玄奉太后之命出迎。他

measures. They decided to organize a group of assassins to ambush Liu Bei in the Temple of Sweet Dew, and assigned General Jia Hua to be the commander. They were determined to kill Liu Bei no matter what took place at the meeting between Wu Guotai and Liu Bei.

When Qiao Xuan arrived at his home, he sent a messenger to deliver some black hair coloring to Liu Bei and instruct him how to use it, so that he would appear at least ten years' younger than his present age. In addition, Liu Bei was warned of a possible ruse being carried out at his expense during the meeting, and was advised to have his generals wear armor inside their military robes in the event a fight should break out.

The great hall of the Temple of Sweet Dew was all arranged for a banquet, with bright red table cloths and chair covers. Naturally, the center seat was reserved for Wu Guotai, and the seat of honor beside her for her future 'son-in-law'. Ceremonial guards and court offcials were all busy decorating the hall, setting out wine and fruit, and arranging the tables and chairs. At the same time, generals and soldiers wearing civilian dress were also busy secreting swords and knives in strategic places in the corridors and wings of the temple. Jia Hua flitted about observing the activities taking place in the front hall; he was in full armor and well-equipped with whips, cudgels and swords; with his hand he constantly fiddled with a large knife.

At this moment, Wu Guotai arrived, accompanied by Qiao Xuan, and was led to her seat of honor. Liu Bei arrived shortly afterwards. Exquisite music echoed through the palace hall.

紧紧握住刘备的双手，细细地看他那染得乌黑的胡子，笑了，小声地说："那上面坐的就是太后，你见了可就要下拜啊！"鼓乐声中，刘备只是会意地点头。

"你是当今的皇叔，我怎能生受得起？"也许是例行的客套话，国太依旧稳稳地坐在那里。这时候乔玄插话了，"太后，新姑老爷过门，总是要拜的。"又转向刘备，"皇叔要多拜几拜！"

刘备懂得怎样满足上座老妇人的自尊心，也深知一位皇叔下拜的分量和能够产生的效果。他严肃地、毕恭毕敬地行了大礼。在端坐上面的太后看来，这实在是一种醉心的享受。接着又引见了赵云。太后对一切都很满意，同时也开始感到孙权和周瑜办事的荒唐，越想越不对劲，朝下面看看，这位二千岁竟到现在还不曾露面。"宣二千岁！"太后说。

孙权上殿参见了母后，勉强向刘备拱拱手，心里有说不出的不耐，好像嚼了一嘴肥皂似的。

谈话转到新姑老爷的身世上来，太后有兴趣地打听，刘备不慌不忙的讲述他的家谱、经历，乔玄不时插进来加一些

Following Wu Guotai's orders, Qiao Xuan stepped forward to greet Liu Bei. He clasped Liu Bei's hands tightly and examined his dyed beard. Qiao Xuan was pleased and whispered to Liu Bei, "That's Wu Guotai seated there. You ought to bow to her!" Liu Bei nodded knowingly.

"You are the present Emperor's uncle. How can I possibly accept such a great honor?" Perhaps in response to this polite formula, Wu Guotai remained seated there with extreme calmness. Then, Qiao Xuan broke the silence, "Your Royal Highness, it's only proper for our new groom to pay his respects to you." He then turned to Liu Bei and said, "It's only polite for you to offer several additional bows to her."

Liu Bei knew how to satisfy the King Mother's sense of self-esteem; he also understood the significance of his bows and the effect they would have. Therefore, he bowed in the most solemn and respectful fashion, which pleased the seated Wu Guotai no end. Next, Zhao Yun was ushered into the hall. Wu Guotai was extremely pleased with all that had gone on so far. But at the same time, she was annoyed that Sun Quan and Zhou Yu had arranged things in such a fashion. When she noticed that Sun Quan had not come, she said, "Call Sun Quan!"

When he arrived, he paid his respects to his mother and unwillingly greeted Liu Bei. Sun Quan was so disgusted that he felt like he had swallowed soap.

The conversation now turned to the subject of the new groom's family background. Liu Bei spoke of his family tree and his experiences in a calm and unpretentious manner. Occasionally, Qiao Xuan would chime in with some additional

注解。太后听得津津有味，孙权则简直有点坐不下去了。

乔玄夸赞了刘皇叔的家世、相貌，"龙眉凤目，两耳垂肩，双手过膝"；在孙权看来，这正是"大耳贼"的注脚。关羽、张飞、赵云的英勇战绩、凌云义气，在乔玄嘴里件件被说得真是神乎其神，这哪里是孙权听得下去的，先还不过警告他少说两句，养养自己的老精神；后来说到诸葛亮借来东风，火烧赤壁的时候，就再也按捺不住。孙权吼道：

"诸葛亮的大火，烧得你坐在这里这么胡说八道！"

吕范走进来请吴侯发布公文。哪里是什么公文？吕范是等得不耐烦，请孙权出去下令动手。

孙权换上箭衣，佩了花剑，身后跟着全副武装的贾华，加上一串刀手，蹑手蹑脚从廊后出发，探头向殿上张望，一队人马随着孙权行进，就像一条花蛇，盯着他的眼色，摩拳擦掌，看见他身边宝剑已经开始离鞘，正想大吼一声一拥而入，不料这时孙权却踌躇了。

"贾华！"孙权叫道。

details, to which the King Mother listened with great pleasure. But, all this only enraged Sun Quan further.

Qiao Xuan next praised Liu Bei's facial features, 'He has phoenix's eyes with the eyebrows of a dragon; his ears hang down to his shoulders; his hands extend below his knees.' This meant to Sun Quan that he was nothing more than a 'Big-Eared Crook'. The brave military accomplishments and lofty aspirations of Guan Yu, Zhang Fei and Zhao Yun were lauded to the skies by Qiao Xuan. Sun Quan naturally found this recitation unbearable and first warned Qiao Xuan to talk less and conserve his energy. But when Qiao Xuan went on to relate how Zhuge Liang 'borrowed the east wind to burn down the whole army of Cao Cao under the Red Cliff', Sun Quan could bear it no longer and let out with a mighty roar.

'Zhuge Liang's fire seems to have fried your brain, so everything you say is nonsense!'

Lü Fan entered and requested Sun Quan to issue an official document. An official document? The truth was that Lü Fan had waited too long and was impatient for Sun Quan to lead the attack.

Sun Quan donned an arrow-proof tunic and his long sword. With the fully armored General Jia Hua and a small group of trained killers behind him Sun Quan set out from the back corridor and was met by additional soldiers and horses, forming a line which resembled a long snake. Itching for battle, they watched Sun Quan starting to pluck his treasured sword from its scabbard. They were all ready to make an all-out attack, when Sun Quan suddenly hesitated.

'Jia Hua!'

"在！"贾华握紧了手中的大刀。

"暂退一箭之地！"孙权的声音有些打颤。

"嘿！"贾华长叹一声，长蛇阵又缩回长廊后面。

正是这当口，殿上相亲已经圆满完成，太后指定乔玄做主持婚礼的大媒，选定良辰吉日，加紧筹备。"皇叔"已经转化为"爱婿"了。

在廊下太后赏赐的席面上，赵云并不曾专心吃酒。他听见了兵器碰撞和叽叽喳喳的说话声，也隐隐觑见了刀手的行动。赵云来到刘备身边，附耳说道，甘露寺中四处都埋伏着刀兵。刘备听了转身一下子就跪在太后的膝前。

太后真的生气了。查问是谁这样无法无天，乔玄在一边说，"恐怕又是二千岁的主意。"于是叫来了孙权、吕范，他们自然都说是"不知情"的。只有全副武装的贾华抵赖无效，太后下令推出斩首。新姑老爷却站出来讲情："今日杀了此人，与儿臣花烛不利！"

在向吴国郡主、孙权小妹尚香的寝宫走去时，刘备依旧摆脱不掉一直纠缠着他的危机感。自踏上东吴的江岸以来，

'Yes!' Jia Hua held a long saber tightly in his hand.

'Withdraw the troops for a length of an arrow shot!' Sun Quan's voice quivered with excitement.

'Hey!' Jia Hua sighed deeply, assembled troops and withdrew into the long corridor.

At the same time, Wu Guotai's meeting with her future son-in-law ended triumphantly. Qiao Xuan was appointed to preside over the wedding ceremony, and an auspicious day and hour had to be selected. The 'Emperor's uncle' was about to become the 'beloved son-in-law'.

At the King Mother's banquet, Zhao Yun could hardly keep his mind on the food and drink. He heard the clicking of weapons, the twittering of voices, saw the movements of the killers in the distance. Zhao Yun approached Liu Bei and whispered to him that soldiers and weapons had surrounded the Temple of Sweet Dew. Liu Bei turned around and kneeled down in front of Wu Guotai.

Wu Guotai became extremely angry, and asked who was acting in such an unprincipled manner. Qiao Xuan said, 'I'm afraid this was our Royal Highness' idea.' Thus Sun Xuan and Lü Fan were summoned to the hall of the temple, though they denied any knowledge of the affair. But Jia Hua's denial came to nought, and Wu Guotai ordered him decapitated. Liu Bei stood up and pleaded for him, 'Killing this person on such a day as today is unpropitious!'

While walking towards the bedroom of his bride Sun Shangxiang, Liu Bei could not rid himself of the sense of danger which had been plaguing him. Ever since he arrived in the Kingdom of Wu, it seemed that traps were set to ensnare

就觉得这地方似乎处处都是陷阱。就连参加了大婚的盛宴，向新房走去的当口，还是死死拉住赵云不放。

赵云从诸葛那里接下的军令是保卫刘备，但宫禁森严，他是不能随便进去的。

一抬头，刘备看见宫门前面排列得整整齐齐的刀枪剑戟的闪烁寒光，在盏盏红灯中间，恰似两排冰柱。刘备不禁冷了半截，难道这是新房中应有的装饰么？

赵云抽身走掉，只剩下了刘备自己。

打开宫门的女侍发现了站在门前发呆的贵人。

盛装端坐在寝宫，秉烛相候的孙尚香，听说新贵人要求先撤去刀枪才肯进来时，不禁微笑了。

"厮杀了半生，怎么还怕这个。"

吴侯孙权的妹妹、郡主孙尚香匆匆接受了太后为自己安排的亲事。她当然不知道自己曾经被当作美人计中的香饵，只是从新婚之夜，新贵人身上透露的某些迹象，向她吞吞吐吐诉说的心事，多少猜到了这桩明显带有政治性质的婚姻背后隐藏着的种种神秘事实。她是聪明的，虽然没有参与国政，但对吴国的处境安危是关心并有兴趣的。这就是她为什么对刘皇叔从一开始就有着好感的原因。不过他为什么见了自己日常习武使用的那些兵器竟如此害怕呢？真可笑。他又为什么在新婚之夜首先向妻子说明处境的危险要求自己庇护呢？他说得多么可怜——

him at each step he took. He kept Zhao Yun at his side at all times, even during the wedding party.

The mission entrusted to Zhao Yun by Zhuge Liang was to protect Liu Bei. But the rules were rigid, and Zhao was not allowed free access to the palace.

Liu Bei was greeted at the palace gate by rows of knives, their icy radiance glimmering in the red lamplight like two rows of icicles. He thought to himself, 'Is it any way to decorate a bridal chamber?'

Zhao Yun left and Liu Bei was completely alone.

While the court ladies opened the palace gate, they beheld their new master standing in a trance.

The sumptuously dressed bride, Sun Shangxiang, was seated in her bridal chamber holding a lantern. She smiled when she was informed that her husband refused to come in unless the armored palace guards withdrew.

'He's spent most of his life in the battlefield; now he's afraid of this?'

Sun Shangxiang readily accepted the marriage her mother had arranged for her. But it wasn't until the wedding night that she learned she was being used as political bait. From her husband's hesitant manner, she could guess there was more to this marriage than met the eye. Shangxiang was smart; though she didn't participate in state affairs, she was greatly concerned about the safety and well-being of the Kingdom of Wu, and for this reason, she was well disposed towards Liu Bei from the very beginning. But why was he so afraid of ordinary weapons? And why did he talk about the dangerous situation he was in and ask for protection?

"我飘泊半生，四海为家。今日得配郡主，三生有幸，只是令兄孙权，每每设计害我……"

她只能搬出太后这座靠山使刘备同时也使自己宽心，不过她也知道，政治上突起的风云变幻，有时并非婚姻的纽带所能维系得住。他们新婚日子过得是幸福的，但又明白这幸福并不是十分牢靠的。

被称为"周郎"的吴国水军都督周瑜，是不久前在赤壁击败了曹操战功卓著的统帅、威望出众的名将。围绕着孙权、周瑜形成了东吴少壮派统治势力。在设法夺回荆州的谋划中，他们设下的美人计遭到了挫败，并受到太后的申斥和元老重臣的抵制，不能不改变策略。在周瑜看来，既已弄假成真，缔结了孙刘之间的婚姻，正不妨将计就计，在宫中广种花木，教习歌舞，使刘备快快活活地住在东吴，消磨了意志，忘却了荆襄，这就能瓦解这个战斗实体的斗志，创造夺回荆州的条件。这是一个更为毒辣的策略，付诸实施时更是顺理成章不会导致任何方面的反对。

刘皇叔甜蜜欢快的新婚日子，像流水似的过去了。

赵云却感到非常的寂寞。他一个人住在馆驿里，已经许久不曾见过刘备。他时时记起临行之前，诸葛托付给自己的

'I have been a wanderer most of my life, and never had a home to call my own. It is my greatest fortune to marry you today, but the one thing that worries me is that your brother Sun Quan is trying to kill me ...'

Sun Shangxiang could only rely on Wu Guotai to offer them protection. But, the political situation changed every minute - something beyond the control of their marriage. They could live very happily together, but they both knew that this happiness was not necessarily permanent.

Zhou Yu, the leading admiral of the Kingdom of Wu, had displayed his extraordinary skill in the battle of the Red Cliff where Cao Cao was defeated. Thus, he and Sun Quan spearheaded the recovery of Jingzhou. Their plot of entrapment had met with objections and was rebuked by Wu Guotai and the senior statesmen and high officials. Therefore, changing their plans became inevitable. From Zhou Yu's point of view, the once make believe marriage had become a reality, so they'd better make the best of a bad thing. The new plan was to embellish the palace with all sorts of luxuries, and assign more court ladies to dance and sing so that Liu Bei would become indulgent. This would gradually sap his will and make him forget all about Jingzhou. This sinister design would be easy to carry out and unlikely to meet with any objections.

Their joyful married life went on as peacefully as a running stream.

Zhao Yun was lonely living by himself. It had been a long time since he had last seen Liu Bei, and he never ceased thinking about the responsibilities entrusted to him by Zhuge

重任，并明确指示年终之时要护卫主公一起回转荆州。光阴易逝，眼看已将岁暮了。

赵云决定进宫去问安。

走进门禁森严的后宫，赵云听到了隐隐箫鼓之声，阵阵后宫女侍的歌声喧笑。他仿佛进入了别一天地。赵云被留在外殿等候了许久，觉得不是滋味。在这陌生的环境中他感到局促、不安。他在殿上来回踱步，活动着自己的肢体，他猛地记起，已有许久不曾跨上战马，挥舞刀枪了。

刘备好像是被女侍们从筵席上拉了出来的，踏进殿门时还兀自与跟随的宫女调笑。

看到站在殿上、神色异常的赵云，刘备睁大了眼睛。

"四弟，你还在这里，没有回去？"

"主公没有吩咐，我能上哪里去呢？"

"回荆州去啊！"

"我不敢离开主公身边。"

刘备失笑了，"你尽管回去，告诉二弟、三弟还有军师，就说我在这里过得好，好，好。要他们放心就是。"

"主公不回去，谁来料理军国大事呢？"

"自有诸葛先生。也许你在馆驿里住得无趣，我这里有的是宫娥彩女，你就选了去作伴也好。"刘备不耐烦了，背过了

Liang: to protect Liu Bei, and to return to Jingzhou by the end of the year. Now, it was almost time.

Zhao Yun decided to go to the court to see his master.

When he entered the heavily guarded rear palace, Zhao Yun heard the faint sound of flutes and drums and the singing and laughter of the court ladies. He felt as if he had entered a strange new world. Zhao Yun waited alone in the entrance hall, feeling cramped and uneasy in this strange place. He paced back and forth, stretching his limbs, and suddenly realized how long it had been since he had last sat astride a war-horse, or executed military exercises.

Giving the appearance of having been dragged away from a feast by the court ladies, Liu Bei was still flirting with them when he stepped through the gate of the hall.

When he saw Zhao Yun standing there with a look of discomfort on his face, Liu Bei was shocked and said,

"Brother, why are you still here?"

"Without your orders, where can I go?" Zhao Yun replied.

"Back to Jingzhou!"

"I cannot leave you alone here."

"But you must go," Liu Bei said with a smile. "Tell our other brothers and Zhuge Liang not to worry about me."

"If you don't go back, who will handle the military and state affairs?"

"Let Zhuge Liang take over. You must be bored all alone in the guest house. There are so many beautiful court ladies and delightful maidens here, why don't you pick a few out to accompany you!" Impatiently, Liu Bei turned around to leave. Zhao Yun had never been snobbed in this manner before. He

身。赵云还从未得到过这种冷遇。他记起，刘备过去也有时
发火，不过从未有这样的严重。他好像换了另一个人，跟过
去的生活完全脱了节。

赵云在思索，用什么方法才能使刘备从精神失常的状态
中解脱出来呢？他知道自己没有这本领。

在寂静中冷场。准都不说话，只有从便殿传来的乐音轻
轻地回荡着。突然，乐音换了一种短促的旋律，急管繁弦，听
了使人格外心焦。这时，赵云猛地想起，只有诸葛才有使刘
备从沉迷中警醒的方法，可他又远在天边。不，他人虽远在
天边，但他的锦囊却安稳地藏在自己怀中。

赵云背过身去，轻轻解开胸前铠甲，探手取出锦囊，仔
细看了，脸上漾出了得意的微笑。赵云转过身来，凑到刘备
耳边，轻声说道："先生差人来报，说那曹操要报当年赤壁之
仇，带领人马，又夺取荆州来了。"

孙尚香听见赵云求见，贵人出去半响不见回来，心里不
免狐疑。赵云已经许久没有进宫，没有大事料他不会冒然进
见。难道是出了什么意外么？

婚后温暖欢快的生活，逐渐医好了刘备精神上的不安，
这一阵子他很少或简直没有提起留在荆州的诸将，也不再担
心东吴少壮派对他的威胁了。这一切，孙尚香是满意的，她

remembered that Liu Bei occasionally got angry and lost his temper, but it was never as severe as this. Now he was acting as if he were another person, as if he had completely cut himself off from the past.

Zhao Yun wondered how he could rescue Liu Bei from this abnormal situation. But he knew there was nothing he could do.

The awkward silence between them was suddenly broken by a stirring tune played by the court musicians. This music seemed to make Zhao Yun realize that only Zhuge Liang could save Liu Bei from further dissipation. Although Zhuge Liang the man was far away; his wise counsel was hidden in the embroidered purse.

Zhao Yun turned around, gently loosened his armor, removed the pouch, and carefully read the second strategy. Smiling broadly Zhao Yun walked to Liu Bei and whispered in his ear: 'Zhuge Liang sent me a message saying Cao Cao is seeking revenge for his defeat at the Red Cliff. He is now leading an army in the direction of Jingzhou.'

Sun Shangxiang learned that Zhao Yun had come to see her husband and became suspicious when he failed to return. Zhao Yun had been away from the court for a long time, and if something important hadn't happened, he would not have come at all.

Their warm, happy married life had gradually cured Liu Bei's anxiety. He seldom mentioned the generals who were still camped at Jingzhou, nor did he worry about the threat from the younger faction within the Kingdom of Wu. Though Sun Shangxiang took great pleasure in her married

到底放下了一颗悬着的心。不过她也时时受着良心的责备，新婚夫婿能为了一个女人，即使是一位郡主，而从此抛却他经营了半生的事业吗？她是不该为此自私的。她并非是一个凡庸的女性，男人的戎马生活一直使她神往，和刘备的结合又逐渐使她明白，她已经开始和他的事业结合在一起了。

刘备和荆州目前似乎已经失去了任何联系，如果这中间还存在着一根纤细的线的话，那就是赵云。现在，这根线又牵动起来了。

孙尚香向前殿走去时下意识地放慢了脚步，这样，她在无意中听到了刘备与赵云悄声的对话。他们正在商量怎样离开东吴回返荆州。行前应否告知郡主，对此他们之间发生了争执。赵云认为一旦郡主知道了他们的意图，就将再也走不成；刘备痛苦地轻声呼喊了："郡主，我刘备要逃走了。"这呼喊不能不使孙尚香听了心碎，她几乎挪不动沉重的脚步。她在前殿看见了失神丧魄的刘备，语言失次，神色仓皇，几经盘问，刘备才说出曹操进攻荆州的消息。孙尚香是清醒的，她并不知道有什么诸葛的锦囊，但她知道这只是一种借口，更使刘备吃惊的是，孙尚香在这时下定的决心。

"皇叔既以国事为重，待我禀知母后，与你同行。"

刘备扑过去跪下，埋头在郡主的膝前，啜泣了。

life, she was constantly feeling pains of conscience over the fact that Liu Bei had sacrificed his entire military career for her sake. Was there any reason for her to be proud about this? Shangxiang was no ordinary woman; she had always been charmed by military life. Her happy marriager to Liu Bei made her realize that her own life was inextricably tied up with his career.

It appeared that at the time Liu Bei had no contact with Jingzhou; in this respect, Zhao Yun would be the only hope. Now that Zhao Yun had returned, it appeared like this connection was coming back to life.

Sun Shangxiang slowed her pace so that she would be able to overhear Liu Bei and Zhao Yun's conversation. They were discussing how to return to Jingzhou, and whether or not they should tell Sun Shangxiang about it. Zhao Yun believed that once Sun Shangxiang found out, they would never get away. Liu Bei cried out, "my princess, I must flee!" Liu Bei's words stung Sun Shangxiang's heart, and she could hardly move. She observed Liu Bei in the front hall; he looked absentminded and panic-stricken, and was speaking incoherently. After repeated inquiries, he told her that Cao Cao was attacking Jingzhou. Although Sun Shangxiang knew nothing of Zhuge Liang's wise counsel, she was clear-minded enough to realize that what Liu Bei said was only an excuse. But what surprised Liu Bei the most was Sun Shangxiang's immediate decision.

She said, 'Since you are so concerned about the fate of your kingdom, I will accompany you after I report to mother.'

Liu Bei threw himself at Sun Shangxiang's feet and began to sob.

尚香进宫辞别母亲，她哪里说得出这极可能是生离死别的辞别，只说要陪同皇叔去江边祭扫；等太后发现了她脸上的泪痕与悲楚之后，经过进一步盘问，尚香才说出了真话。母亲也并未阻拦女儿的去意，等她哭泣着辞别了老母，迟疑地向外走去时，母亲又唤她回来。"你们这次回去，必须经过柴桑口，那周瑜怎肯放你们过去？"

太后将一口上方宝剑递给女儿，"中途有人拦阻，就可斩却，凡事都有为娘做主。"母亲知道女儿和新婚是留不住的，也不应该把他们永远留在自己身边，毅然放他们去了。伏在母亲膝前哭泣的孙尚香知道自己到底是母亲锺爱的女儿，可是她那掌管东吴军政大权的哥哥呢？她真的是吴侯的亲妹子么？

周瑜是个精明的人，三十四岁就成了军事统帅，赤壁一战，奠定了东吴的基业也树立了自己的威信。他和鲁肃都是主战派，也是孙刘联合政策的具体执行人。只是年少气盛，不肯服输，一贯凭自己想当然的意图行事。他设下的"美人计"失败了，使他懊恼、傍徨。他自娶了乔公的小女儿成为孙吴的外戚，从此踏进上层，一直一帆风顺，他遇到的是一连串

When Sun Shangxiang went to take leave of her mother, she could not intimate that this might be her final farewell, but said instead that she was going to accompany Liu Bei to the river bank to sweep their ancestors' graves. However, seeing her daughter's face covered with tears, Wu Guotai pressed Sun Shangxiang for the truth. After learning the real reason for their journey, Wu Guotai gave her daughter her approval, and they parted in tears. Just as Sun Shangxiang was walking out, her mother called to her, 'You will have to pass by Chaisang on this trip; perhaps Zhou Yu will not let you out!'

Wu Guotai presented her daughter with an imperial sword and said, 'If anyone tries to block your way, you may kill him. I will personally bear the responsibility.' Sun Shangxiang kneeled down before Wu Guotai, knowing that she was still her mother's beloved daughter. But she wondered if she was still the sister of the man who handled the military and state business of the Kingdom of Wu?

Zhou Yu was an astute man. He had been a military commander since the age of 34, and in the battle of the Red Cliff, he laid both a foundation for the Kingdom of Wu and established a high reputation for himself. He and Lu Su were both in favor of war, and were instrumental in arranging the cooperation between Sun and Liu in the battle of the Red Cliff. Zhou Yu was a young man with a vigorous spirit and a reluctance to admit defeat; he always acted according to his own will. The failure of the entrapment plot annoyed him no end. Since he had married the younger daughter of Qiao Xuan, he became a relative of the Suns; from then on everything had

成功，他提出的战略计划，从没有碰过壁，可是这回第一次事与愿违，失了面子。这是不能不使他懊恼的。

他发现站在自己面前的敌人增多起来了，霸占了荆州的刘备，倒成了东吴的"娇客"；那个一直沉着冷静、时常露出不怀好意的微笑的诸葛亮，就更加可恶。尤为糟糕的是，本来和自己站在一起的鲁肃，最近也经常提出不同的意见来了。不仅要对付外来的敌人，还要留神在内部蔓延开来的不稳思想。花了很大力气也说服不了的鲁肃，简直就像一根僵死的木头……周瑜开始感到在这内外交困之中，有些精力不济，又更增添了烦躁、不安，容易发火，怎么用力也很难控制得住。

为了掩盖自己的失误，挽回威信并统一内部认识，周瑜宣布他正在执行一种新的策略，把刘备用目前这种特异的方式永远囚禁起来，分散他的集团力量，进而加以分化、各个击破，进一步完成收复荆州的大业。孙权是将信将疑地被说服接受了，鲁肃就一直说不通。周瑜自己也不免觉得有些口硬心软，刘备是个活人，而活人是很难一直加以有效的"圈禁"的，何况他的身份还是东吴的"娇客"、"贵人"。

周瑜像往常一样，升帐理事。他处理着日常的军机事务，显得从容不迫，保持着大将、统帅的威严、风度。统帅部设

proceeded smoothy, and all his military strategies were carried out with success. Only this time, when things went against his wishes, he could not help but feel that he had lost face.

Zhou Yu could see his enemies multiplying before his very eyes. The man who had seized Jingzhou had become the 'son-in-law' of the Kingdom of Wu, and then there was cold-hearted Zhuge Liang, whose smiles couldn't conceal his malicious intentions. The worse thing of all was that his partner, Lu Su, who had always concurred with him, had recently come up with differing opinions. So now he was confronted not only with external enemies, but by antagonistic currents within the ranks. He had already put much effort into talking Lu Su over to his side, but he remained as immovable as a tree. Under these circumstances, Zhou Yu's feelings of helplessness intensified to the point where they were becoming hard to control.

In order to conceal his weak position, revive his personal prestige, and resolve internal contradictions, Zhou Yu announced that he was carrying out a new strategy: Liu Bei would be imprisoned in the Kingdom of Wu for the rest of life; his military forces would be dispersed, enabling the Kingdom of Wu gradually to dissolve the strength of the Kingdom of Shu and achieve the goal of recovering Jingzhou. Suspended between doubt and belief, Sun Quan was finally persuaded to follow Zhou Yu, but Lu Su had never given in. However, Zhou Yu was smart enough to realize that keeping Liu Bei in captivity was a bad plan in the long run, particularly since he had already become a 'son-in-law' to the Kingdom of Wu.

Zhou Yu carried out his duties in a leisurely fashion yet with dignity of a great general. His headquarters were located

置在柴桑，这是控制通往刘备集团根据地的咽喉地带。近日来他加紧了巡逻和侦察，对来往行人严格进行盘问。要防备从荆州方面可能来袭的武装力量，也注意不让任何奸细出入国境。对这方面的戒备，他是满意的，可是又并不安心。

不祥的消息终于来了。刘备带了郡主已经向荆州逃去。周瑜一跃而起，正待点兵亲自追赶，鲁肃一脚踏进帐来。"那刘备带领郡主同回荆州，有什么不是，为何要派兵追赶？"

"好不容易才把他诓过江来，怎能轻易放他走掉！"

"只怕太后不会答应。"

"自有吴侯作主！"

"荆州发兵前来？"

"自有本督抵挡！"

"那诸葛亮可不是好惹的啊！"鲁肃最后冲口而出了。

争论还是旧的争论。鲁肃过去一直不愿也不敢提起，他知道什么是最能揭开周瑜疮疤的旧事，谁是最使周瑜厌恶、并深深忌惮的人，此刻也还是说了出来。鲁肃当然拦阻不住周瑜。一支追赶刘备一行的人马出发了。

周瑜派出先行的追兵，由丁奉、徐盛等四将统率，他们最先遥遥地望见了刘备一行的车尘马迹。这一群显然走得十分慌促，出发以来一直没有停下来休息过，显然都已十分疲惫了。远远望去，刘备骑了马先行，后面跟着郡主的车辆，断

at Chaisang, a place of strategic importance near Liu Bei's forces. Missions of inspection and reconnaissance become more frequent, and all who passed by the headquarters were subject to interrogation in order to prevent spies from crossing the border. Zhou Yu was quite satisfied with these arrangements, but he still felt uneasy.

Bad news came at last: Liu Bei and his wife were on their way to Jingzhou. Zhou Yu jumped when he heard the news; while the soldiers began to assemble, Lu Su stepped into Zhou Yu's tent and said, 'There is nothing wrong with Liu Bei bringing his wife back to Jingzhou. Why are you sending soldiers after them?'

'It was difficult enough getting him to come to Wu. How can we just let him go so easily!' Zhou Yu replied.

'I'm afraid the King's Mother would disagree with you,' said Lu Su.

'Sun Quan would certainly back me.'

'What if troops are being sent out from Jingzhou?'

'I would be in charge of the defense.'

'Zhuge Liang isn't easily provoked.' Lu Su said without hesitation.

This was a familiar argument for both of them. Lu Su had never dared stir up unpleasant memories in Zhou Yu, though he did mention the name of the one person Zhou Yu detested the most. Lu Su could do nothing to stop Zhou Yu, and a group of soldiers and horses set off after Liu Bei and his party.

Ding Feng and Xu Sheng were two of the four generals leading the troops. They first saw Liu Bei's carts and horses hastening forward in the distance; though because they had not rested since setting out, the pace of the group seemed to

后的是赵云。看来他们已经发现了追兵，明白不容易摆脱，逐渐放慢了前进的速度。丁奉等正迟疑时，被追蹑的一群已经在前面的山坡上停下来了。

丁奉他们也跟着停了下来，一时还不敢凑近去。

在山坡上歇下以后，赵云知道已到了打开诸葛最后一封锦囊的时机。诸葛教给刘备，目前只有请孙夫人出面解围，硬挤是不明智的。

孙夫人款款地从车中走出。她掠了一下鬓发，安详地站在那里，像是在眺望风景似的望着远处的追兵。赵云侍立在一旁，手里捧着太后赏给的上方宝剑，刘备则远远躲在后面观看动静。

丁奉他们牵了马慢慢地走近来，在山坡下面停下，恭谨地参拜了郡主，却用眼睃着刘备。

"丁奉、徐盛、蒋钦、周泰，"孙夫人依次威严地唤着四将的名字，"你们来干什么？"

"奉了吴侯之命，请皇叔与郡主回去。"这是出发之前周瑜教给他们的。

"嘟！"孙夫人放下了脸，"你们奉了吴侯之命，可我奉的是母后的懿旨，与皇叔同返荆州。"她回头给赵云递了一个

be slowing. Liu Bei, on horseback, led the group, followed by Sun Shangxiang's cart. Zhao Yun brought up the rear. They had most likely noticed the soldiers, and realizing how difficult it would be to break away from them, finally halted on the slope.

Ding Feng also ordered a halt, but was hesitant about making an instant attack.

Zhao Yun knew this was the right time to read Zhuge Liang's final message of wise counsel. The message was to have Sun Shangxiang rescue them from the siege, since the fight at that point would have been unwise.

Sun Shangxiang dismounted from her cart. Brushing aside the hair on her forehead with her hand, she stood there calmly, viewing the distant troops as if she were enjoying a beautiful natural scene. Zhao Yun, standing by her side, was holding the imperial sword given to her by Wu Guotai. Liu Bei hid himself behind them in a place from where he could see everything that was going on.

Ding Feng and his troops led their horses forward and stopped at the foot of the slope. They paid homage to Sun Shangxiang, but did not fail to notice Liu Bei.

'Ding Feng, Xu Sheng, Jiang Qin, Zhou Tai!' one by one, Sun Shangxiang majestically called out the four generals' names. 'What are you here for?'

'We are here with orders from Sun Quan. Your Highness and your honorable husband are requested to return.' These were the words Zhou Yu had entrusted them with before they left.

'Though you are under orders, we are making this trip back to Jingzhou with the blessings of the King Mother.' She turned

眼色，"赵云，请出母后钦赐的上方宝剑，有胆敢阻拦的就给我杀了。"

丁奉等只能眼睁睁地看着刘备他们上马，登舆，从山坡上离去。最后离开的是赵云，他冷笑着在马上挥舞宝剑，像是向送行者告别。

丁奉等回去时碰上了随后赶来的周瑜。用不了好久，以周瑜为首的追兵又追上了刘备一行。依旧是孙夫人出场，周瑜也说不出更强有力的理由，只不过重复了刚才发生过的一切，与诸将不同的是，周瑜和赵云交了手，但不敢厮杀，最后还是眼看着刘备他们从架起的宝剑下面走掉了。

即使是都督，也不能不忌惮这上方宝剑。

都督的对策还是追，追。周瑜把希望寄托在面前不远的长江。

一只小船从茫茫无际的芦苇丛中摇了出来。

站在船头上的是张飞。混身黑色的渔夫装束，脚踏麻鞋，头上戴了一顶镶着黑边的圆圆的大草笠。他的双眼闪闪的，黝黑的脸膛上泛出了因激动而生的飞红。他等在这里好久了，不时探头望望辽阔的江面和蜿蜒的江边小路。好不容易才盼

around and winked at Zhao Yun. 'Zhao Yun, show them the imperial sword presented to us by the King Mother. Whoever dares to block our way will be killed.'

Ding Feng and his followers could only stand there and watch helplessly as Liu Bei mounted his horse and rode off. Zhao Yun was the last to mount, and rode off with a sneer on his face, wielding the imperial sword, as if saying good-bye to a group of friends seeing him off.

On the way back, Ding Feng's group met with Zhou Yu's which came up from behind. And shortly afterwards, Zhou Yu's soldiers caught up with Liu Bei's party. For a second time, it fell upon Sun Shangxiang to step forward and speak, and what followed was a mere repetition of what had gone on before. Zhou Yu failed to present any better reasons to justify his actions, and only ended up battling one-to-one with Zhao Yu. Though there were no casualties, Liu Bei's group made up while their swords were still clashing.

Even a high official like Zhou Yu was rendered powerless by that imperial sword.

Pursuing Liu Bei seemed to be the only way to deal with the situation, and Zhou Yu put his last hopes on the nearby Yangtze River.

A small rowboat emerged from the nearly endless patch of reeds growing in the river.

The man standing on the bow, Zhang Fei, was dressed like a fisherman in black clothing, and had on straw snadals and a round straw hat edged with black. His eyes glistened, and his dark face was flushed with excitement. He had been waiting there for a long time, gazing over the vast expanse of river and

到了遥远扬起的尘头，按照自己的经验，知道这是一起行进中的车马，他还不能断定这是不是他奉命迎候的远来贵客。

刘备一行终于来到了周瑜最后希望所寄的大江。

刘备站在滔滔的江水面前，回头望着远处即将追近的周瑜兵马，觉得真的陷于绝境了。

是赵云先发现了从苇荡中闪出了一点黑色的影子，紧接着又是一点、两点，它们箭似的向岸边驶来，这时可以看清这是一串乌皮小艇。前面并排行进的两条，渐渐逼近，可以看见诸葛亮手中的白色羽扇了。

这是一场意外惊喜的会见。其中最活跃的是张飞。他抚弄着胸前飘拂的长须，跳来跳去招呼这个，又问讯那个，正如一个小孩子。这些时，一直没得到大哥的消息，也数他最焦急沉不住气。他几次闹到诸葛亮帐前，讨下了江边迎候的任务。他带了三千人马，乔装改扮，隐伏在苇荡中，等得不耐烦，曾不止一次在失望之余动摇了对诸葛亮的信心。难道他猜得就这么准？现在，也是他来到诸葛亮面前，挑起拇指，称赞他的聪明的预见；在赵云那里，张飞又夸赞了他保卫大哥安全归来的功绩。最后刘备引他与新嫂嫂相见，老张不禁腼腆起来，他走过去嗫嚅着下拜，孙夫人嫣然一笑，说，"三弟少礼！"张飞还是第一次看见这般神采飘逸的人物，听

the winding paths along the river bank. Finally he noticed curls of flying dust in the distance. He knew this signaled the arrival of horses and carts, but it was too early to judge whether these were the important guests he was expecting.

Liu Bei's party finally arrived at the big river, where all of Zhou Yu's hopes lay.

Standing on the bank, Liu Bei turned around and saw Zhou Yu's troops approaching and felt that the end was near.

Zhao Yu first noticed a few black shadows in the reed bushes. As they grew larger, it became clear that they were a group of small bark boats. Finally Zhao Yun could see that it was Zhuge Liang, holding a white feather fan in his hand.

This was a most unexpected surprise, particularly for Zhang Fei. He fondled his long beard, which hung down to his chest, and bounced about like a child, greeting and chatting with those who had just arrived. He was also greatly concerned with his brother-in-arms Liu Bei. How many times had he appealed to Zhuge Liang before the master strategist finally promised him the job of receiving Liu Bei. Zhang Fei led 3,000 soldiers and horses disguised as fishermen, and took cover in the reeds. Impatience led him to lose confidence in Zhuge Liang, but finally when everything turned out just as Zhuge Liang predicted, he made a special visit to praise Zhuge Liang's brilliant foresight. Zhang Fei spoke highly of Zhao Yun's efforts in escorting Liu Bei back safely. Later, Liu Bei took Zhang Fei to meet his bride, and he shyly kneeled down to pay his respects. Sun Shangxiang smiled at him winsomely and said, 'There's no need to be so polite!' Her grace and beauty came as a pleasant surprise to Zhang Fei, who had never met such a

到陌生而使人心醉的吴侬软语,老张向身边人做了一个鬼脸,轻轻地学说了句,"三弟少礼!"没有谁听得清楚张飞嘴里咕哝些什么。

诸葛亮安排新婚夫妇下船,又对张飞交代了任务。一瞬间江边又恢复了平静,江水照旧滔滔地向东流去。战斗在前面不远的山坡下发生,周郎这次遇见的不是太后的上方宝剑而是张三爷的丈八蛇矛。他知道自己是彻底失败了。山坡高处排列着一队黑色衣装跳跃着的兵士,他们欢快地、齐声高喊:

"周郎妙计安天下,

赔了夫人又折兵!"

这也是诸葛亮的安排,恰似事先做好的一份简洁、确切的战役总结。

person before. Her sweet-sounding voice was intoxicating to him, and he turned to someone beside him, made a funny face, and tried to imitate her voice; but nobody understood what he was mumbling about.

Zhuge Liang arranged for Liu Bei and Sun Shangxiang to get a boat, and handed the task to Zhang Fei. In a twinkling, the river became quiet again. A war broke out at the foot of the slope not far from the river. What confronted Zhou Yu at this time was not the imperial sword of Wu Guotai, but Zhang Fei's long serpent spear. He knew though that he would fail miserably. In the meantime, at a higher point on the slope, there was a group of soldiers dressed in black and assembled in rows, who were jumping about and shouting with delight:

Zhou Yu thought he had a plan,
To take the whole world in his hands.
He failed to snare with feminine charms,
And finally lost in the contest of arms.

This was a perfect reflection of Zhuge Liang's straregy, and made a neat conclusion for the little battle.

空城计

三国（220—265）后期，由曹操子孙统治的魏国实力逐渐增强，而以诸葛亮为相的蜀国渐渐变弱。正在那时，魏军在司马懿统率下出其不意进攻魏蜀接壤处的一城池。蜀相诸葛亮完全没有时间布防，遂定下空城之计，令魏军相信城中有重兵埋伏，不进而退。故事见诸于长篇小说《三国演义》，在中国尽人皆知。

在中国，人们常常将具有预知能力或者足智多谋的人誉为"诸葛亮"。

——编者

诸葛亮有些疲倦了。这些年北伐的战争对蜀国来说已成为一种沉重负担，对他个人来说就尤其如此。近来他是日益感到自己是在干着一件将永远不可能完成的工作，可是他只能努力干下去。这些年他一直是强打精神来办事，在全蜀军

The Ruse of the Empty City

During the latter period of the Three Kingdoms (220-265) the Kingdom of Wei, which was ruled by Cao Cao's descendants, was increasing in power while the Kingdom of Shu, governed by Zhuge Liang, was getting progressively weaker. Just at this time, the commander-in-chief of the Wei army, Sima Yi, marshaled his troops to attack a city in Shu located near the border between the two kingdoms. Completely taken off guard by this surprise attack, Zhuge Liang, the minister of Shu, had no time to prepare an adequate defense of the city. Famous for his resourcefulness in military strategy, Zhuge Liang devised the strategy of deceiving the Wei troops into retreating by making them believe that the besieged city was defended by a large army. This incident, which is recounted in the novel The Romance of the Three Kingdoms, *is well known to all Chinese people.*

In China, if someone has prophetic powers or is extremely resourceful, he is often referred to as being a 'Zhuge Liang'.

-Ed.-

Zhuge Liang was a little weary. These last few years the military expeditions against the north had become a heavy burden on the Kingdom of Shu - and weighed particularly heavily on him personally. He had recently begun to feel that he was engaged in an impossible job, yet he knew that he must keep working at. These last few years he had to make an extra

民文武百官看来，丞相依旧是精力弥满的。可是他自己明白，他的体力衰退得厉害，胃口、饭量也日益减弱，当他从大堂点兵出发，退回自己的私室，一屁股坐下来时，就像一滩泥似的，不想动，也几乎不能动了。

可是他的脑子依旧静不下来。这次出兵的整个计划，从制定到实施，确是花了不少力气。他把大将赵云派到襄城去，吸引开魏军的注意，亲率主力指向了祁山。魏军派来拒战的是有经验的宿将张郃。他考虑了很久才选派了马谡作前军统帅镇守街亭。马谡是老资格的参谋人员，先帝在世时就一直参预军事策划，很有学问，也出过不少好主意，加上他在自己身边很久，对自己的军事思想是熟知的，只是缺少实战的经验。在万不得已的情况下派了他去独当一面，至少可以保证不会干出荒唐幼稚的事来。他这样想着时，多少放下了心，这时就留神看看左右，没有人。身边两个年轻的随从懂得丞相的脾气，丞相喜欢一个人在内室休息，不愿意旁人打扰。他是在休息么，也很难说。随从不敢进来也不敢走远，得随时

effort to brace himself in order to get things done. To the people and soldiers, scholars and officials of Shu, their Prime Minister appeared to be full of vim and vigor; but he himself was well aware that he had lost much of his energy, and that his appetite was worsening daily. When he returned to his inner room from the hall, he would slump down into his chair, unwilling - and nearly unable - to move.

But still his mind could not relax. The planning of this latest campaign – from formulation to implementation– had seriously taxed his energies. He had sent General Zhao Yun to attack Xiang Cheng in order to divert the attention of the Wei army, and would then personally lead the main forces towards Qishan Mountain. Appointed by the Kingdom of Wei to lead its resistance force was the veteran general Zhang He. Zhuge Liang pondered deeply before deciding to send Ma Su as commander of a forward division to garrison Jieting. Ma Su was an experienced advisor, who had always participated in the planning of military strategy for the late emperor. A deeply learned man, he had put forward many valuable ideas. In addition, he had cooperated with Zhuge Liang for years and was familiar with his military strategies. His only shortcoming was a lack of practical experience. Sending him out to take command of the operation was a last resort, which would at least ensure that no naive moves would be made. This notion made Zhuge Liang more at ease, so he diverted his attention by looking around him. But there was no one in sight. His two young attendants understood the Prime Minister's temperament, and knew that he liked to rest alone in his inner room. Was he actually resting? It was difficult to say. His attendants dared

听候呼唤。有时也偷偷从门缝里张看一下，常常看见丞相在房里来回踱步，手里拿着那把时刻不离的羽扇，有时停下来举起扇子来瞧，一瞧半日，仿佛那上面有什么花样似的。有一次小随从偷偷瞧过那把扇子，只见黑白间架的鹅毛美丽花纹，看了一眼就赶紧放下了，什么花样都看不出。

这时候，诸葛亮真的又在房里来回踱步了，手里依旧拿着那把扇子。不过没有看，他有时停下来抬头望着房顶的天花板。其实那里也是空落落的，顶梁上缀着老大一面网，一个大蜘蛛静静地坐在网上休息，一动不动。

诸葛亮在想什么呢？他总是忘不了马谡接下军令时脸上的笑。马谡平时不是这样的。也许他这是第一次接受独当一面的重任，有点激动吧，也许不是。诸葛亮不禁有点担心。接着又赶紧安慰自己。出发前，已经把地形、扎营方法、作战序列都细细地对马谡说了，简直把这有了一把胡子的将军当作一个小孩子。这是诸葛亮的老脾气。马谡也满口答应着去了，可是从脸上也看得出，他没有听进去。想想马谡对自己还一直都是顺从的，因此也就理应没有什么可以担心的。

neither to enter the room nor to wander too far. They were ready at all times for his summons. Sometimes they would peep through a crack in the door and see the Prime Minister pacing up and down the room, holding the feather fan which never left his hand. Sometimes he would intently gaze at it as if examining an intricate design on its surface. Once one of his young attendants secretly looked at the fan, but all he could see was a beautiful arrangement of black and white goose feathers.

Now Zhuge Liang was once more pacing the room with fan in his hand, but he wasn't looking at it. Occasionally he would pause and stare up at the ceiling, although it was quite empty save for a huge old spider web suspended between the rafters, with a large spider resting peacefully in its center.

What was Zhuge Liang thinking about? He was recalling the smile on Ma Su's face as he received his orders. Perhaps Ma was a little excited at being given the responsibility of commanding a contingent of infantry and cavalry for the first time, but, on the other hand, perhaps not. Zhuge Liang couldn't suppress a rising suspicion, but quickly consoled himself. Before setting out, Zhuge Liang had discussed in great detail the terrain of the area and its surfance features, as well as the method of striking camp and the battle order to be adopted, explaining these things to the bearded general as if he were a small child. This was one of Zhuge Liang's peculiarities. But although Ma Su agreed readily to everything he proposed, it could be seen from his face that he had not absorbed what was being said. But Ma had already left, and in the past he had always obeyed his directions, so there should be nothing to worry about.

就这样，诸葛亮在房里一个人呆了好半日，吃了饭，喝了茶，也不想上床去歪一歪；不知怎的，好像全部精神都提了起来，一点都不困。就这样，眼看着日色平西了。

诸葛亮心里盘算，马谡带着大军出发，走了半日，该已到了街亭。按照自己的部署，派出哨兵，察看地形，安营扎寨。这一切粗粗安排好，就动手画地理图。这用不了多少时间。然后派快马送图回来，这当儿，也许至多再晚一刻，就该到了。可是大营内外依旧静悄悄的，一点声音都没有。诸葛亮得意地微笑，这是他长期治军形成的纪律。即使身边带着几万、十几万大军，照样也是这么静悄悄。不过很快又想到，他的兵全给赵云和马谡带走了，这回的静悄悄是真正的静悄悄，他只有时听见几个老兵的咳嗽声，压低着嗓子，可是听来依旧清晰得很，也寂寞得很。

约莫在掌灯以后许久，诸葛亮才听见了从远处逐渐移近，急遽，匆促，零乱的马啼声。他放下了心。直到他开始背着手从摇摇的烛光下看那打开来的草草画就的地形图时，他脸上还浮着微笑。他看这样的地图是老手了。他不是从头到尾细细地看，只是选择了几个地点注视。三眼两眼，他的眼睛不由得张大了，接着就闭起了眼睛，手一挥，就又快步走回房里去了。

Zhuge Liang remained in his room for a long time. He ate and drank but felt no desire to rest. Unaccountably his spirits had soared and he was not in the least sleepy. He watched the sun set.

In his mind's eye, Zhuge Liang followed Ma Su setting out at the head of his army, completing the long journey and arriving at Jieting. According to his own instruction, guards would be posted, the local terrain would be surveyed and camp pitched. They would then begin on a map of the area which would be sent back to Zhuge Liang by fast horse. At the latest it should arrive in another quarter of an hour. The main camp remained peaceful and quiet, both inside and out. There was not a sound to be heard. A complacent smile touched Zhuge Liang's face. This was discipline borne of his own long-term administration of the army. Even if his own camp had contained hundreds of thousands of soldiers, it would still be just as quiet as this. But he quickly recalled that all his soldiers had been led away by Zhao Yun and Ma Su, and that this time the silence was real. All he could hear was the occasional muffled coughing of a few old soldiers, the sound clear and lonely in the night air.

It was only after the oil lamps had been lit for some time that Zhuge Liang heard the distant clatter of horses' hooves gradually drawing near. He relaxed and smiled as he examined the roughly drawn topographical map lying before him in the flickering candlelight. He was an old hand at reading this kind of map, concentrating his attention on a few select areas. With a wave of the hand, he dismissed the map and returned swiftly to his room.

第二天早晨，天刚麻麻亮，诸葛亮就从房里走了出来，他走过这个小城静悄悄的狭窄荒凉的街道，穿出城门，向城外一片平展的麦地了望，麦地中间有一条不宽的土黄驿路，蜿蜒着一直望不到头。这就是大军出发走的那条路，也是昨夜送地图的快马驰过的路。他料准了将在这里迎来一骑混身淌汗的探马。他一点都不惊异，平静地听取了"马谡失守街亭"的坏消息，甚至连眉头都没有皱一皱。他缓步走回来，又穿过城门，走上了城楼。在城门洞口看见两个老兵时，还向他们微笑。老兵心里希奇，丞相今天高兴。这是多年来罕见的，好像只有那年平定了南中，收服了孟获，班师时曾经这样笑过。

诸葛亮一个人站在城头向远处望去，望了好久。

他觉得整个战役已经结束了。他觉得可惜了花了年把时间努力进行的准备工作虚掷了。他觉得惭愧，战争失败的关键就在他用错了前军主将。他感到困难，主要的困难并不在撤军，摆脱司马懿的追兵，这些昨夜就早已盘算好了。他细细算过，损失可以减少到最低限度。最困难的是大军退回川中以后的善后，怎样处置马谡、还有他自己。他是没有退路

The next morning the sun had barely risen when Zhuge Liang left his room. Walking through the silent city along the narrow, desolate streets, he went out through the city gate and stood gazing into the distance at the flat wheat fields before him, and the narrow, yellow-earth post road that twisted and turned out of sight. This was the road that his armies had set out upon and the road that the speeding pony carrying the map had traversed the night before. As he imagined, he met here a sweat-soaked scout horse, and listened in a calm and unruffled manner to the bad news that Ma Su had been unable to hold the garrison at Jieting. He walked slowly back though the city gate and climbed the gate tower. Meeting two old soldiers in the gateway he smiled faintly, making them wonder why the Prime Minister was happy today. He had not smiled like that since the time when Nanzhong was pacified, the allegiance of Meng Huo was won back and the troops had returned home in victory.

For a long time Zhuge Liang stood alone on the wall gazing into the distance.

Zhuge Liang felt with regret that the entire campaign was over. The long preparations had been cast aside for nothing. He felt ashamed. The deciding factor in his defeat had been the misuse of the chief commander of his forward contingent. There were difficulties ahead, but the major difficulties lay not in withdrawing his army and throwing off the pursuing armies of Sima Yi - this had been solved the evening before, and he calculated that losses could be cut down to a bare minimum. The greatest difficulty lay in problems that would arise after the army had retreated to Chuanzhong. How should he deal with Ma Su? And what about himself? He really had

的，不能辞职，更不能不继续经营准备北伐，不出击就只能坐待敌人来消灭。怎样才能维持住并继续激起蜀国军民的战斗热情呢？

诸葛亮两眼望着碧蓝的天空，天上有白云。这地方会变成一个战场么？许多往事都一下子袭来。马谡的命运早就决定了，在第一次看到那地形图时就决定了。使诸葛亮感到十分不安的是，是谁把马谡推进死亡的深渊的呢？是张郃吗？不是。想来想去，只能是丞相他自己。在弥留的病榻上衰老苍白的刘备的面容仿佛又在云端里显现了。"谁教你这样使用马谡的，我不是几次提醒过你，这个人是不能独当一面的么！"他仿佛听见了刘备微弱却又愤怒的声音，看见他脸上因激动而泛起的潮红。

诸葛亮拿着羽扇的右手微微颤动，他闭起了眼睛，口中喃喃地说着什么，没有谁能分辨得出。他是在祈祷，求先帝帮助他度过难关，改正错误。他睁开双眼，眼前依旧是一片澄澈得出奇的碧蓝的天。

诸葛亮吩咐随从，转命老兵，要把城门内外、城头一带打扫得干干净净，还要准备琴桌、酒菜，他自己要在这里吃

no way out. He could not resign, even less could he refuse to continue to direct the preparations for the expedition against the north. If he did not attack, he could only wait for the enemy to come and annihilate his army. How could he hold out and continue to rouse the fighting spirit of the people and army of Shu?

Zhuge Liang gazed into the deep blue sky. Would this place become a battlefield? Several past events suddenly flashed into his mind. Ma Su's fate had been determined very early with the first glance at that topographical map. What made Zhuge Liang so uneasy was the question of just who had pushed Ma Su into the deep waters of destruction and death? Was it Zhang He? After much thought he concluded it was the Prime Minister himself. The pallid face of Liu Bei seemed to appear before him in the snow. 'Who told you to send in Ma Su as commander? How many times did I warn you that he cannot handle such a responsibility!' He could hear Liu Bei's weak but angry voice and see the red flush of agitation on the old man's face.

Zhuge Liang muttered something to himself that no one could understand. He was praying to the late emperor for help to get through this crisis and correct his mistakes. When he opened his eyes, the same expanse of brilliantly clear blue sky still lay before him.

Zhuge Liang instructed his attendants to order the old soldiers to sweep all the streets inside and outside the city gates and around the city walls. Then he ordered them to prepare some snacks to eat with wine and bring him his *qin* (a musical instrument resembling the zither). He had decided to drink a little, play his *qin* and admire the scenery. To his

酒、弹琴,观赏风景。他对睁了呆呆双眼的年轻的随从说,"你们看,这里的风景多好,看那远山……"

诸葛亮一开始就作了最坏的打算。他估计司马懿得到张郃夺取街亭的消息,调集兵力袭击西城,这需要两天时间。不过应该估算司马可能还会来得更快,不需要这许久。他又向远处望了一望,没有一点马蹄踏起灰尘的迹象。就算他来得更快一些,又怎样呢? 诸葛亮一下子产生了非凡的自信。他研究、了解司马的深度,实在远远超出了对马谡的认识。他感到有些惭愧,但坚信,这一回,他不会也不许再犯错误了。

从接连来到的探马带来的消息,知道司马懿的队伍确已向西城进发。这消息,在诸葛亮少量留守人员身上引起的反应是不同的。诸葛亮缓步走下城楼时又遇见了那两个曾经跟他渡泸南征的老兵,丞相微笑着对他们说:

"你们辛苦一下,把城里城外打扫一遍,越干净越好,"接着又和解似地说,"就在这里左近扫扫就行了。那边么,不必了。"他举起羽扇,指着城隅一侧拥挤着一片破烂屋舍和残砖碎瓦的角落,脸上又出现了微笑。

一切都不出诸葛亮的预计,但也不是都估算得那么准。

incredulous young attendant he explained: 'Look! The scenery here is so beautiful. Look at that mountain … '

From the start, Zhuge Liang was prepared for the worst. He guessed that as soon as Sima Yi heard the news that Zhang He had seized Jieting, he would immediately assemble his forces and make a surprise attack on West City. This would take a minimum of two days. But he also considered the possibility of Sima Yi's arriving more quickly. He gazed off into the distance, but there was no sign of dust raised by horses' hooves. If he did arrive more quickly, what could be done anyway? Zhuge Liang suddenly felt a great surge of self-confidence. The depth of his understanding of Sima Yi far exceeded his knowledge of Ma Su. He felt a little ashamed, but firmly believed that this time he would not make any more mistakes.

From the intelligence constantly being brought in by his scouts, Zhuge Liang knew that Sima Yi's troops were already advancing on West City. This news evoked quite different reactions from Zhuge Liang and from the small number of garrison troops left in the city. Zhuge Liang climbed slowly down the gate tower and met two old soldiers with whom he had once crossed the Lu River on an expedition south through Sichuan. He said:

'You really must make an effort to sweep the town clean, the cleaner the better. Sweep this neighborhood to the left; there's no need to sweep those areas over there.' He pointed with his fan towards tumbledown slums crowded into one corner of the city. A slight smile touched his face.

As it turned out, nothing exceeded Zhuge Liang's expectations, but he was not entirely correct either. Sima Yi's

司马懿的大军比他保险系数打得很高的估计来得还要快。一些老弱残兵刚把城门左近清理了一下，探马就报告说，"司马懿的大兵离西城不远了。"

诸葛亮又急匆匆地走上了城楼，但没有人看得出他内心的不安。他像一个典型的名士那样在城头就坐，像阮籍那样地喝酒，像嵇康那样地弹琴。这些司马懿都从部下的报告里详细地了解到并暗暗吃惊了。司马懿的坐骑停在一个小土坡上，离得远，地势却高，他看不大清楚，但可以断定那坐在城头上的人只能是诸葛亮。他见过大世面，知道这种潇洒的风度和舒缓飘逸的琴音不是第二个人能有的，这是地地道道"正始"的风格，模仿不来的。司马懿在马上踌躇了好半日，终于下令退兵。他不想参加诸葛亮的音乐酒会。这可不是联欢的恰当时机，诸葛亮也不像是一位好客的主人。司马懿想了好久，终于下了决心，"回去！"

诸葛亮坐在大堂上，显得无比烦躁。这实在是少有的。半月来他"演戏"演得够了。他盛怒地处分了前军副帅王平，十足地发了一顿脾气。他为胜利地完成了掩护撤军任务的老将

armies arrived even sooner than he had anticipated, even allowing a very high safety margin. A few crippled old soldiers had just finished cleaning up the streets around the left side of the city gate when a scout arrived to report: "Sima Yi's army is now close to West City!"

Zhuge Liang hastily reclimbed the gate tower, but no one could see any sign of anxiety in his mind. He sat like a scholarly eccentric on the city wall, drinking wine and playing his *qin*. Sima Yi knew all this in detail from his subordinates' reports, and the news made him inwardly alarmed. He reined his horse to halt on a small slope, still a long way from the city. He couldn't see clearly, but he was certain that the figure seated on the city wall could only be Zhuge Liang. He had had much experience of the world and knew that such a natural, unrestrained deportment and leisurely elegant manner of playing the *qin* could belong to no other man. This was the highest expression of the style and manner of the "Zhengshi" period of the Kingdom of Wei, and could hardly be imitated. Sima Yi hesitated for a long while on his horse and finally gave the order to retreat. He did not feel like taking part in Zhuge Liang's wine and music party. This was not the appropriate moment for a friendly get-together, and Zhuge Liang was not likely to be a hospitable host. Sima Yi thought for a long time and finally made up his mind : "Go back."

Zhuge Liang sat in the hall looking highly agitated - a very rare sight. In the last two weeks he had acted out many roles. He had angrily punished Wang Ping, the deputy commander of the forward army, bringing into play the full weight of his anger, and had commended the veteran general Zhao Yun for

军赵云庆了功。但当免冠散发、带着手铐、满脸晦气的马谡被押上堂时，诸葛亮却意外地平静了下来。他知道，现在来了对他说是最严重的考验。

马谡像是一只低着头，被斗败了的公鸡。过去他脸上那一派骄矜之色一点没有了。他的声音喑哑了，他服罪，承担了全部责任，他不希望万一的侥幸。这一切都使诸葛亮心烦。如果马谡耍态度，强调客观困难，撒泼打滚，那倒要好办些。但马谡不是这样，诸葛亮不能不想，整个的悲剧好像是一个做成的圈套，又是身为丞相的他亲手推着马谡钻进去的。是他要马谡签署了军令状，他的知人之明到哪里去了呢？

他淡忘了军事法庭的尊严，不由自己地从座上走下来，走到跪着的马谡身边，他想对马谡说两句什么，这时他看见马谡失神的眼睛里饱含着泪水。他一下子忘记了想说的话。死一样沉寂的大堂上，前后左右肃立着的全军将佐、士兵，全部的眼睛都盯着他看，一对对竖起的耳朵都在听。好一会，先是轻轻的，然后愈来愈高，一阵阵压低了但使人听了发颤的声音打破了死一样的寂静。诸葛亮惊慌失措了，这是他平生仅有的一次失仪，他偷偷向四周扫了一眼，慌促地溜回自己的座位，很快地，简直可以说是草率地宣布了处决的命令。

covering the retreating army. But when the hatless and disheveled Ma Su was forced into the hall, his hands shackled and his face despondent, Zhuge Liang suddenly became calm. He knew that this was going to be his most critical trial.

Ma Su was like a defeated rooster in a cockfight. The proud and haughty air he had always worn in the past was gone. His voice was dull and hoarse. He admitted his guilt and accepted full responsibility, not even blaming his defeat on ill luck. This all made Zhuge Liang feel very vexed. If Ma Su had lost his temper and stressed the difficulties he had faced, it would have been easier to handle his case. But Ma Su was just not like that. Zhuge Liang could only think that the whole tragedy was a trap into which he as Prime Minister had forced Ma Su. It was he who had wanted Ma Su to sign the military orders. Where had his famed insight into people's characters and capabilities disappeared to?

The dignity of the military court faded from his mind and he rose from his seat and approached the kneeling man, intending to say a few words to him. Only then did he see that Ma Su's dispirited eyes were brimming with unshed tears. He forgot everything he was going to say. In deathly silence, the whole army of officers and men stood ranked around him, every eye upon him, every ear strained to listen to his words. Then faintly at first, but soon louder and louder, wave after wave of suppressed murmuring broke the silence. Zhuge Liang was panic-stricken. This was the first time in his life he had lost his usual manner. His eyes swept the court room and he hastily escaped back to his seat. Quickly - one could even say perfunctorily - he issued the order for execution.

醉酒

　　杨玉环原是唐明皇儿子寿王的妃子。唐明皇见她貌美，先让她出家当道姑，再将她纳入宫中为妃，并将对后宫三千佳丽的宠爱集于她一人身上。

　　该剧讲述杨贵妃在百花亭等候皇上，准备与皇上同饮。

　　梅兰芳上世纪三十年代在美国演出该剧，他扮演的贵妃酒醉的身段、神态之美难以描绘，完全征服了美国观众和剧评界。

　　该剧是京剧梅派的保留剧目。人们一说起京剧，便立即会想到梅兰芳和他最具代表性的角色：《醉酒》中的贵妃。

——编者

　　高力士在沉香亭畔看着宫女们在调排案几，安置盆花，准备酒果、宫烛，跑前跑后，指指点点，不停地挥动着手

The Drunken Beauty

Yang Yuhuan was originally the consort of Prince Shou, a son of the Tang Emperor Minghuang. Emperor Minghuang discovered her beauty and first had her made a Taoist priestess and then afterwards took her into the palace to be the highest ranking imperial concubine, his favorite among 3,000.

This Opera recounts the story of how Yang waited in the One Hundred Flower Pavilion for the emperor to arrive in order to drink with him.

When Mei Lanfang performed in this opera in the United States in the 1930s, his portrayal of the gestures and attitudes of the drunken concubine was so superbly convincing that it literally surpassed description, and was widely acclaimed by American audiences and theater critics.

This opera is a standby in the repertoire of actors in the Mei Langfang school of Beijing Opera. One need merely mention Beijing Opera and people will immediately think of Mei Langfang, and his most representative role is that of the tipsy concubine in the opera The Drunken Beauty.

-Ed.-

Next to the Pavilion of Deep Fragrance, Gao Lishi watched attentively as the court maids laid out the banquet table, set pots of flowers about and prepared the wine, fruit and candles. He rushed around giving orders and continually

中的牙柄麈尾。虽然刚交初夏，额头竟自沁出了细细一层汗珠。

当时正是大唐的极盛时期，天下太平，域内丰足，边境安谧。明皇几乎把全部精力都花在女宠游乐上面。唐宫里正是朝朝宴乐，夜夜元宵，一片鲜花着锦的繁华景象。好像人间的快乐已经再也装载不下，要漫过高高的宫墙，涨溢到外面来了。但高力士心头却没来由地浮上了一层细微的不安。好似太液池头传来了阵阵隐约雷声，不知道是否会带来一阵雷雨。

明皇几乎有半月光景没有和杨玉环在一起饮宴了。当然谁都知道那原因，但谁也不肯说。今天贵妃吩咐备酒时的神态，语气也有点古怪。为什么不在殿里而偏偏选上这沉香亭？高力士不喜欢这地方，他在这里出过丑，可是他没有猜到，这正是杨玉环选上这地方的原因。她是想借这里的名花、台榭唤醒明皇对往事的回忆，记起她们曾在这里度过的好时光，记起李白写的《清平调》，记起明皇自己说过"赏名花，

whisking the ivory-handled duster in his hand. Though it was only the beginning of summer, beads of sweat covered his forehead.

It was the heyday of the Great Tang Empire. The country was at peace; its coffers and granaries were full; its frontiers were secure. Minghuang, the reigning emperor, spent nearly all of his time indulging in wine and women. Within the palace, it was festival delicacies morning after morning, New Year dumplings night after night, brocade and flowers everywhere. It seemed that the palace could no longer contain so many worldly pleasures, which would soon spill over the high walls into the world beyond. But for some unknown reason, Gao Lishi's thoughts were a bit cloudy. He fancied hearing a rumble of thunder from the direction of Taiye Pool. Was a storm brewing?

The emperor had not wined or dined with Lady Yang Yuhuan, his favorite, for nearly two weeks. Of course, the reason for this was well known, but no one would mention it. Today, when the imperial concubine gave orders to prepare wine, her voice and manner were somewhat strange. Why was the rendezvous not being held in the palace but in this out-of-the-way pavilion? Gao Lishi did not like this place, for he had once made a fool of himself here; but he did not know that this was the very reason why Lady Yang had chosen the place. She hoped that the famous flowers and the pavilion and terrace would awaken the emperor's memories of the past - memories of good times spent together, the poem set to the song *Qingping Melody* that the great poet Li Bai wrote here, and the emperor's own words, '... enjoying the flowers face to

对妃子"的话……这个小女人在当前小小的尖锐斗争中的确费了心机，不过到底还拿不准有几分把握。

杨贵妃穿上了盛装，由宫女们簇拥而来，脸上一片喜悦的睛光，可是没有谁理会这中间也出现过偶然一闪的阴影。她带着矜持的微笑看花，路过玉石桥时看水里的金鱼和懒懒偎依在一起的鸳鸯，好像这一切都非常新鲜。她缓缓地来到御案前就坐，瞥了一眼身边空着的并排的另一副宝座。她在心里叮嘱自己要沉住气。宫女们捧着份内的执事,高力士、裴力士眼睛看着地面，按仪注一一站在各自的位置上。好长啊，这等候圣驾来临的时刻。

那是昨天，杨玉环退朝时在宫里迎候皇帝，抽空在玄宗耳边提出今晚在沉香亭夜宴。玄宗脸上漾着笑，静静地听着。近来玄宗脸上新添的这种捉摸不定的神色，给她带来很大的苦恼。她好像失去了什么，再也拿不住他了。她明白引起这种变化的原因，她想通过主动的努力，重新扇起玄宗心头日趋衰颓的情热。这是一个冒险的试验，就看他来不来了。

当知道玄宗今晚终于不会到来，御驾是向梅妃居住的西

face with my favorite ...' The little lady had taken great pains in the petty feud that was now going on; still, she could not be sure of the outcome.

Dressed in her finest gown and escorted by a procession of maids, the imperial concubine appeared on the scene sailing broadly; though nobody noticed the shadow that occasionally passed across her face. With an air of dignity, she looked at the flowers along the way; when passing over the Jade-and-Stone Bridge, she paused to observe the goldfish and the mandarin ducks as if all these things were very fresh and interesting. Slowly she approached the imperial table and sat down, at the same time casting a glance at the empty seat beside her and counseling herself to remain calm. The maids busied themselves with their tasks while Gao Lishi and Pei Lishi, eyes fixed upon the ground, stood in their places fixed by court etiquette. It was going to be a long, long wait for the arrival of His Majesty.

The day before, after court had adjourned, Lady Yang met the emperor in the palace and seized the opportunity to whisper to him her request for the banquet tonight in the Pavilion of Deep Fragrance. The emperor only smiled in silence. Of late, she had been much worried by this strange new expression on his face. She felt as if she had lost something and would never hold on to him again. She knew the cause of this change and hoped that through her initiative she could rekindle in his bosom the passion that was dying away. It was a risky venture; the outcome of which depended on whether or not he would appear tonight.

The bitter news arrived. The emperor would not be coming;

宫转去时，杨玉环失去了最后的矜持。她下令，"待娘娘自饮几杯。"她要报复，她不再想在奴才面前挽回失尽的面子，她需要的是失去更多的面子，这面子、尊严并非只属于自己，似乎也不应由她单方面加以维持了。

虽然并排的一双宝座上只孤单地坐着一位娘娘，太监和宫女们还是恪守着惯例一巡巡地上来敬酒。酒也有种种名色，如龙凤酒，这是因皇帝和贵妃同饮得名的，现在却只能由她自己独饮；通宵酒，是要彻夜长饮的，但对手又在哪里呢？杨玉环起先还用手中的扇子遮住酒盏送到唇边；随后就丢开了扇子，学男子那样的轰饮；到后来索性从高力士手中抢过酒杯，灌下喉咙。她酒后燥热，站起来打算脱下身上的凤衣，就在欠身时双腿发软，几乎站立不稳。她一手扶着案边，向赶来搀扶的宫女轻轻摇头微笑，为自己的不胜酒力解嘲。

脱下凤衣，换上宫装的杨玉环，蓦地看见阶前盛开的盆花，她想去嗅花。她得俯下身子才能亲近那艳丽的花朵，太

his imperial carriage was headed for the West Palace, the residence of Lady Mei. Lady Yang lost her last reserves of dignity. She gave orders that she would have a few drinks by herself. She sought revenge. No longer caring about restoring the 'face' she had lost, what she wanted was to lose even more. After all, the question of face and dignity was not her business alone. Why should she try to resolve it by herself?

Though one of the two seats of honor that stood side by side was empty, the eunuchs and maids served up course after course in the prescribed manner. There were famous drinks like the Dragon-Phoenix Wine, so named because the emperor and his favorite had enjoyed it together. Now she was to drink it alone. It was to be an all-night banquet at which the wine was to flow until dawn. But where was her drinking partner? At first she affected coyness and would hold up her fan to conceal the cup each time she put it to her lips; soon, however, she threw the fan aside and drank in huge gulps like a man; eventually she went so far as to snatch the cup from Gao Lishi's hands and pour the contents down her throat. The excess drinking made her feel hot and dry, and she stood up to remove her phoenix robe. She had only half risen when her legs weakened and she found she could hardly stand; but she held on to the table with one hand, smiled and shook her head at the maids who rushed up to help her. She was trying to cover up her incapacity for drink.

After removing her phoenix robe and putting on a court dress, Lady Yang turned to admire the flowers blooming in pots on the terrace. She wanted to smell the blossoms, but to do so she had to bend down. The eunuchs and maids

监宫女们担心地看她摇摇地蹲下身子，不敢劝阻，不敢搀扶，看她像走出梦境似的眯着迷离的双眼，知道她确是醉了。

可是她依旧唤人再斟上酒来。

太监和宫女们跪在地上用金盘捧上了酒盏。杨玉环就像嗅花似的俯身在盏中啜饮，还衔杯仰身不留下一点余沥。她终于沉沉地醉了。

杨玉环倚着亭槛昏昏地入梦了。

只不过是旧年的春天，依旧是这沉香亭畔。今天她却只能在梦里追回那阵阵欢笑，新谱成的《清平调》歌声和李三郎饧着眼的醉态了。李三郎，这玄宗的小名，只在两种情况下她才能使用，才敢使用。一种是她爱极了的时候，还有就是恨极了的时候。她记起在寿王邸里，就是被饧着眼的李三郎第一次看中，接下去就来了那一连串抹不掉的欢笑的日子。今天她是第一次感到一切都是那么脆弱，不可靠。既然宠爱是可以转换的，不长久的，那么还有随同宠爱俱来的一切呢？

梦中的时光像箭一样快，梦里的关山也是能举足飞越的；人世间的忧乐荣辱在梦境中的转换也特别来得快。杨玉环像跨上了一匹无缰的野马，一下子就跑到了深渊的崖角。正当

watched with concern as she stooped, but none dared stop her or offer a hand. Seeing her with the bleary, half-closed eyes of one who had just walked out of a dream, they knew she was far gone.

Yet when she turned around, she called for more wine.

Kneeling, she eunuchs and maids offered her a small cup on a gold platter. She bent down and sipped it; then, holding the cup between her teeth, she threw back her head and drained it to the last drop. She was dead drunk now, and leaning in a stupor against the balustrade, was soon in the land of dreams.

It was only last spring, at this very same pavilion, that amid peals of laughter she listened to the new poem composed to the tune of the *Qingping Melody*, and enjoyed watching 'Third Brother Li' getting drunk. Now this was all a dream. 'Third Brother Li' was the emperor's pet name which she dared to use only when she loved or hated him intensely. She recalled how she first caught the emperor's fancy in the home of Prince Shou. This was followed by unforgettable days of rejoicing. But today, for the first time, she realized how frail and insecure their love was; if the passionate love she had experienced could be passed on to another, what about the other favors that came along with it?

Time in dreams flies like an arrow: mountains can be crossed in one stride; and secular joys and sorrows, honor and dishonor, succeed each other in rapid sequence. Lady Yang felt as if she were riding an unbridled horse that was carrying her swiftly to the edge of a cliff. Just as she was about to call for help, she woke to find Gao Lishi and the others on their

她要喊出声来时，高力士们已经跪在面前轻轻地撼着她的双膝，一面嗫嚅着报道，"圣驾来了！"

酒一下子醒了一半，精神也陡长了。她很快地站起来，宫女们一下子来到身边，怕她站不稳。她们跟跄地一起下了亭子，来到花径旁边，照规矩跪下，伏在地上。杨玉环不敢相信这一切是真的，不是梦。她埋头在宫装的长袖里，长久地俯伏着，抱着满脸的惭愧与畏惧，不敢抬头去看那可能已站在面前的李三郎。

杨玉环就这样在地上伏了很久。

等她知道这一切全是骗局，是高力士们为了把她从沉醉中唤醒想出的骗局时，她嗒然了。她呆呆地望着跪在面前谢罪的一群太监和宫女，这些算不得人的人们，忽地感到了难以支持的疲倦，酒涌上来，身子软瘫了。她给宫女们架着，也许是抬着拖着，一步步挨回了寝宫。

这时夜已将半。在静悄的后宫里，从西苑传来的箫鼓歌声格外清亮。这不是《霓裳羽衣曲》，准是新填成按谱的歌子。杨玉环在沉醉中自然没有注意，但落入高力士耳中时，不禁也引起了一点轻微的愤慨。

knees before her. Gently shaking her knees, they announced in a halting voice: 'His Majesty is here!'

This was enough to dispel a good portion of her drunkenness and arouse her instantly. Hastily she clambered to her feet as the maids rushed up to help, fearing she would be unable to stand by herself. They escorted her to the flowered path and there, according to custom, prostrated themselves upon the ground. Lady Yang could not believe that what was happening was true; it had to be a dream! Burying her face in the long sleeves of her court dress, she crouched in shame and fear, not daring to lift her head and look at the emperor, whom she imagined was standing before her.

Thus for quite some time she remained there on her hands and knees.

Finally a loyal attendant plucked up the courage to tell her that this was only a trick thought up by Gao Lishi and the others to revive her from her drunkenness. She was stunned. The sorry lot of eunuchs and maids that could hardly be called human were upon their knees again begging her forgiveness, but she stared at them blankly, sensing a sudden unbearable fatigue. The wine took effect again and she was about to collapse. Supported by her maids, she tottered back to her chambers.

It was almost midnight. In the stillness of the inner palace, the drums, flutes, and singing in the west courtyard sounded loud and clear. It was not the familiar *Rainbow and Feathery Garment Dance* they were playing; it was a new poem set to an old tune. Lady Yang in her drunken state did not notice it; but it fell upon the ears of Gao Lishi, vexing him slightly.

穆柯寨

京剧有一个特点，许多历史传奇故事都是根据历史真人撰写的。中国历史上确有杨继业其人（？-986），他是第一代杨家将。不过，有关他后代的爱国功绩和爱情故事可都是戏剧家和作家的虚构作品。

该剧讲述第二代杨家将杨延昭率军抗击契丹入侵者，第三代杨家将杨宗保被穆桂英所擒。穆父原为宋朝官员，时在穆柯寨占山为王。后来杨宗保与穆结为夫妇，共赴前线御敌。

——编者

一员女将，立马在山坡之上。十七八岁年纪，全身披挂，背后端端正正束着四面套旗。她顾盼神飞，眉目间闪露着跳动、变幻，只有小女儿才有的惊喜。她注视着脚下的一片草

The Muke Mountain Redoubt

One of the characteristics of Beijing Opera is that it features many historical romances which include numerous legends based on actual historical figures. Historically, there was indeed a man named Yang Jiye (?-986), the first of the generals of the Yang family. However, the stories concerning the patriotic exploits and love affairs of his descendants are merely the products of the imaginations of dramatists and authors.

This opera recounts the story of how, when Yang Yanzhao, a second generation general of the Yang family, led his troops to resist the Qidan (Khitan) invaders, Yang Zongbao, a third generation general of the Yang family, was captured by Mu Guiying, the daughter of a Song dynasty official who led a hermit's existence in the Muke Mountain Redoubt. Later, Yang Zongbao married Mu Guiying and together they went to the battlefront to help repulse the Qidan invaders.

-Ed.-

The young woman general Mu Guiying appeared on the mountain slope, sitting erect upon her horse. She was a girl of about 17 or 18 years old and wore a full suit of armor. The banners she wore on her back fluttered in regular rows that stretched in all directions. As she looked around, surveying the grasslands and forests below her feet, a lively expression

原、林木。她是为了散心才出来打猎的，原不必穿上一整套出师会阵的戎装。可是她喜欢这样打扮。丫头喊："姑娘，雁来啦！"她头也不回，眼光依旧随着天上的雁群移动，随手从丫环手里接过雕弓。左手执弓，右手搭箭，身儿一侧，中了。那雁带着箭飞去，女将和手下的女兵朝着落雁的方向纵马赶去。

女将并不隶属于任何一支正规国家武装，她是一个山寨大王的女儿。北宋时，这样的山寨大大小小几乎到处都有。多半是受不了赋税、欺凌铤而走险的农民，也有从官宦群中分离出来的人物。穆桂英的父亲，穆柯寨的"天王"穆洪举就曾是宋朝的一名官员，因为朝中奸臣当道，这才退归林下的。这不过是一种好听的说法，其实是占山为王。他身边只有这个锺爱的独生女儿，不只武艺超群，指挥作战也颇有过人的才能。上了年纪的天王几乎把山寨的大小事全都交给了女儿。女儿的任性天真，老天王也无可奈何。对女儿的锺爱，有时

lit up her face. She had come out today to divert herself by going hunting, so she need not have worn her full military battle attire; but she loved to dress up this way anyway. The servant girl by her side cried out, 'Mistress, the geese are coming!' Mu Guiying followed the path of the wild geese that flew across the sky. She took up her carved bow, grasped it with her left hand, and drew back the arrow with her right. She fired and immediately struck a direct hit. The injured goose flew on with the arrow stuck in its belly, and they spurred their horses forward to follow it.

General Mu Guiying did not command the army of any ordinary country: she was the daughter of the ruler of a fortified mountain city. During the Northern Song Dynasty, fortified cities of this type could be found almost everywhere. The majority were occupied by peasants who had fled in desperation from intolerable taxation and oppression, though they also provided a haven for dismissed court officials. Mu Hongju, Guiying's father, was the master of the fortified city of Muke. He himself had previously been an official of the Song court, but evil and treacherous ministers had forced him to flee and hide in the forest. To speak more truthfully, he had forcefully occupied the mountain territory and made himself its ruler. His family consisted of his one daughter whom he loved dearly, and who possessed uncommon skills in the arts of war and in commanding an army, besides numerous other remarkable abilities. The aging ruler had handed over most of the 'affairs of state' into her capable hands. As for the headstrong yet intelligent character of his daughter, the old master could do little to change that. His

几乎变成了溺爱。不过老头儿心里有数,女儿年纪轻,没经过世面,但她心地善良,为人正直。"总错不到哪里去。"自己落得省心。这阵子,他就正好出门闲游去了。

女将一行驰马绕过山头,远远望见树林旁边系着两匹战马,草地上站着全副武装的红、黑两将。一位脸色红得像一团火,他是孟良;另一位黑得像锅底的是焦赞。他们与镇守三关的统帅杨延昭是结拜弟兄,也是杨元帅帐下的得力将领。

是他们拾起了穆桂英射落的雁,孟良从焦赞手里接过从雁身上拔下来的箭,细看精巧的雕翎箭杆上刻下的一行小字"穆桂英百发百中"。

"这是穆桂英的箭!"孟良失口说。他们这次正是奉了元帅的将令,到穆柯寨来找降龙木的。

当时宋辽之间又爆发了战争。辽国的萧天佐摆下了天门大阵。杨延昭正从各地调集援兵,起用战将。命焦赞上五台

love for his daughter at times became almost obsessive. But the old man was no fool, and knew that although his daughter was young and had little experience of the world, she had a pure heart and was honest and upright in her dealings with others. He said, "She would never take a step in the wrong direction." He could rely on her with his mind at ease. Indeed, even now, he had left the mountain to go traveling.

As Mu Guiying galloped on her horse across the mountainside, she noticed in the far distance two war horses and two generals standing on the grass plain in full battle dress. One of them had a face as red as a ball of fire - this was Meng Liang; the other had a face as black at the bottom of a cooking pot - this was Jiao Zan. They were sworn brothers of Yang Yanzhao, the commander-in-chief of the garrison of the Three Passes.

It was they who had picked up the wild goose shot by Mu Guiying. Meng Liang took the arrow that Jiao Zan had plucked from the dead goose, and carefully inspected the words that were finely carved into its shaft: 'One hundred arrows fried by Mu Guiying gain one hundred direct hits.'

'This is Mu Guiying's arrow!' exclaimed Meng Liang. It was precisely in order to see Mu Guiying that their commander had sent them here. They had come to request her to give them the 'dragon-subduing wood'.

At that time, war had once more broken out between the kingdoms of Song and Liao (Qidan). Xiao Tianzuo, from the Kingdom of Liao, was organizing the army battalions, while Yang Yanzhao went throughout the land seeking troop reinforcements and asking retired generals to take up arms

山搬请出了家的五哥前来助阵。杨五郎使用的兵器是板斧，缺少木柄，指定要降龙木制做。这就是他们哥俩远路来到穆柯寨的原因。这降龙木是寨里的镇山之宝。

他们哥俩拿着这箭商议对策，照孟良的意思应该把这箭和打下来的雁一起交还原主，可是焦赞却主张用这作为交换条件，和穆桂英讨价还价，他一把抢过箭来，嘻嘻笑道："降龙木有了。"

正在这时，穆桂英派来讨回落雁的丫环走近来了。

焦赞看出了来的并非穆桂英本人，发话道：

"回去告诉穆桂英，让她乖乖地献出降龙木来。要不，就要踏平你们的山寨！"

接着当然是一场厮打，丫环败阵回去了。

换上来的才是穆桂英。孟良被焦赞拉上马去，心里想，这恐怕不能硬来，不过嘴里刚迸出了一声"穆小姐……"就给焦赞拦了回去。他想用不着这种客套，还是开门见山，把刚

once more. Yang also ordered Jiao Zan to go to Wutai Mountain to ask his fifth brother, who had become a monk, to lend his assistance. Commander Yang's fifth brother wanted to use the 'dragon-subduing wood' to make the handle of his broad axe. This therefore was the mission that had brought these two brothers to such distant lands, for the special 'dragon-subduing wood' was the treasured asset of this strategic mountain city.

The two brothers discussed how to dispose of the arrow that was now in their possession. Meng Liang opined that they should give both the arrow and the goose back to their rightful owner, but Jiao Zan proposed that they should use this opportunity to bargain more effectively with Mu Guiying. He seized the arrow and said, 'The 'dragon-subduing wood' will be ours for sure!'

At this moment, Mu Guiying's servant girl approached to reclaim the goose.

When Jiao Zan saw that it was not Mu Guiying herself who had come, he cried out.

'Go back and tell Mu Guiying to provide us with the 'dragon-subduing wood'. If she refuses, we will destroy your mountain city!'

This provoked a fight between them, but in the end, the servant girl lost and went away.

Mu Guiying then came over in person, whereupon Jiao Zan pulled Meng Liang onto his horse. Judging that this situation should not be dealt with by force, Meng Liang blurted out 'Miss Mu ... ' but was quickly silenced by Jiao Zan. Jiao Zan did not consider such politeness necessary; instead, he came straight

才对丫环说过的话再重复一遍。一言不合，又照样是一场战斗。不同的是，这回给打下马来的是他们哥儿俩，穆桂英得胜以后回山去了。

到穆柯寨来取降龙木，本是焦赞从元帅那里接下的将令。半路正好碰上回营交令的孟良，顺便把他也一起拖了来了。在焦赞看来，孟二哥有时不免过于小心谨慎，不及自己聪敏机变。可惜这回又低估了穆桂英，"你我堂堂大将，被那丫头打下马来，成何体统！"对孟良的发怒与埋怨，焦赞简直没有什么话好说。这时他又有了主意，瞒过元帅，把"小本官"杨宗保请来，"三马连环，何愁女寇不灭！"正在奉命巡营了哨的小将杨宗保果然被两位叔父连激带哄地搬了来。

穆桂英不觉眼前一亮。她还从来没有看见过这样一位白马银枪、威风凛凛的小将，这么出色的人物。穆桂英虽说是"天王"的女儿，从小跟父亲练就一身武艺，可是常年在山里生活，并没有见过外边热闹的世界，不懂什么规矩、礼数，

to the point and simply repeated what he had said to the servant girl. Instantly, another battle ensued. But this time, the outcome was different, for it was the brothers who were knocked off their horses and defeated. After her victory, Mu Guiying rode back into the mountains.

The order to go to Muke had originally come down from the supreme commander to Jiao Zan alone. But along the way, Jiao Zan chanced to meet up with Meng Liang, who was returning to his garrison to report in, and the two of them continued on together. In the eyes of Jiao Zan, Meng Liang was sometimes rather faint-hearted and overcautious and could not compare with himself in terms of intelligence and flexibility. Unfortunately, he had under-estimated Mu Guiying this time. 'Two formidable generals were pulled off their horses by that young slip of a girl. What a disgrace!' Jiao Zan could say nothing in reply to the angry reprimands of Meng Liang. But then he came up with a plan: without informing his supreme commander, he asked Yang Zongbao to come and lend a hand. He was sure that the combined force of three cavaliers would suppress that girl bandit once and for all! The young general Yang Zongbao, at the time under orders to inspect the garrison and the sentry posts, was hence persuaded by the two brothers to come and help them out.

Mu Guiying's eyes lit up at the apparition before her. She had never in her life seen such a dashing and magnificent young man as General Yang Zongbao, mounted as he was on a white horse with a silver spear at his side. Although Mu Guiying was the daughter of a so-called 'King of Heaven', and had practiced the arts of war with her father since childhood,

更没有见过什么出色的人物。和杨宗保一会阵,就使她想起了早年随父亲逛庙在神殿前面看见过的手执降魔宝杵的韦驮。对啦,这不就是韦驮,活了,骑着马下山了。两马交错,穆桂英不住地打量这员小将,盘问他是什么人,到此何事?后来听说他是杨元帅的儿子,上山是为了降龙木时,就说"好哇,你要的宝贝包在我身上啦!""拿来!""跟我到山坡上来!"

她(他)们一直不停地在马上交手,和与焦、孟两将作战时不同,她(他)们打得没有那么急凑,那么疾风骤雨,立时就见分晓。穆桂英总是设法把杨宗保猛刺过来的银枪挡住、架起,找机会细细打量对方,顺便问两句话。这真是一员英勇的小将,可是又多么不懂人情,好像没看见和他交手的是一位姑娘。有时她一发狠,几下就把他逼了回去,可是又哪肯伤害对手,只不过下死劲地盯他一眼,好像说,"看你还发狠!"接着就抿嘴一笑,把马头拨回来了。

杨宗保也觉得有点希奇,他不懂这个女孩子到底是在打

she had never strayed too far from her mountain home to explore the bustling world around her. She understood nothing of the rules of etiquette and had certainly never met any man of outstanding qualities. Yang Zongbao reminded her of the statue of Skanda holding his demon-defying club, which stood in front of the temple she visited with her father when she was a child. Surely this was none other than the reincarnation of Skanda himself, riding down the mountainside. When their two horses met, Mu Guiying scrutinized this young general from head to toe. She asked him his name and the purpose of his journey. When she learned that he was Commander Yang's son. and that he had come to fetch 'dragon-subduing wood', she exclaimed: 'Very well! Leave it all up to me. Come up the mountainside and get them!'

They fought as they rode on horseback. But Mu Guiying did not fight as she had with Meng Liang and Jiao Zan. This combat was much less violent, and the outcome was predictable before they started. As Mu Guiying intercepted Yang Zongbao's lunging silver spear, she was seeking a way to size up her opponent more carefully and ask him a few questions. He was a truly courageous young general, but he appeared to understand very little about human feelings. He had hardly noticed that his enemy was a girl. For an instant, the venom would rise up in her and she would close in upon him, driving him back. But she had no wish to injure him and simply gave him a long look, as if to say: "How could you be in such fury!" and then purse her lips in a smile and pull her horse around.

Yang Zongbao was also rather perplexed by this situation, for he could hardly tell if his young opponent was fighting or

仗还是游戏，她的枪法是厉害的，可是到了紧要关头，就软下来，又把马拨回去了。他定定神，暗暗下了决心，这次一定要把你打下马来。可是又一次打了"平手"。他竟悟不出这是对手对自己的忍让，反而被撩得发起火来。

穆桂英这时已经拿定了主意，把小将引上了山坡，又一次把他逼到了无法回手的地位，"哎！"她紧紧攥了一下手里的银枪，轻轻一挑，杨宗保就从马上滚了下来。她身边的女兵像进行例行公事似的熟练地就把战俘捆起，驮上马背，带回山寨去了。

远远躲在山角的焦赞和孟良这时只有暗中叫苦。

焦赞是不肯服输的。他指着孟良背的火葫芦，撺掇他放火烧山。还说自己会"分火"会掐诀念咒，拘来一条"冷龙"，骑着钻入火塘，把小本官救出来。他们真的烧起了一场漫山大火。有"分火扇"的是穆桂英，她一扇就把焦孟两将煽进火堆里，烧得面目黧黑，须眉燎尽，只好拣起发烫的兵器，回营请罪去。

simply play-acting. She attacked with great ferocity, yet always seemed to draw back at the critical moment. He gathered all his courage and made a secret resolve; this time he would knock her off her horse once and for all. But once again, their fighting resulted in a draw. Yang Zongbao was quite unaware of the purposeful restraint being practiced by his opponent; at the same time, he was roused to anger by her vicious parries.

By this time, Mu Guiying had worked out a plan of action. She led the young general up the mountain slope and once more fought him into a tough corner. She grabbed his silver spear and lightly jerked it upward, tumbling Yang Zongbao off his horse. Thereupon, the assistant at her side came forward and with a well-practiced hand tied up the prisoner. She then raised him onto the back of his horse and took him back to the fortified mountain city.

Jiao Zan and Meng Liang cried out in dismay as they watched the scene from their mountain hiding place.

Jiao Zan was still unwilling to admit defeat. Pointing to the 'fire gourd' Meng Liang was carrying on his back, he suggested they should burn the whole mountain to ashes. He claimed to be able to 'direct the flames' and that by chanting magic incantations he could summon up an 'iee dragon', which he would then ride into the flames and rescue Yang Zongbao. They set the mountain on fire, but Mu Guiying herself possessed a 'flame dividing fan', with which she fanned Jiao Zan and Meng Liang right into the fire, burning their faces black and singeing away their eye-brows and whiskers. They had no choice but to pick up their burning hot weapons and return to their garrison in disgrace.

杨排风

在讲述四代杨家将保卫国家的故事中，家族中的许多女性起了重要作用。杨家的巾帼英雄包括佘赛花、杨八姐、柴郡主、穆桂英等，都是让敌人闻风丧胆的将帅。即使是杨府的一个烧火丫环杨排风，也是一名武艺超群的战将。

该剧的主要目的是让女主人公杨排风展示她精湛的武艺。虽说这是一个战争故事，但全剧诙谐、风趣，让观众获得极大的愉悦感。

——编者

杨排风从三关回来，依旧在天波府大厨房的灶下烧火。她是立了功回来的。按照当时佘太君的将令，杨宗保在边关被辽将韩昌擒去，谁能救得小本官还朝，"高官得做，骏马任

Yang Paifeng

In the story of how the four generations of generals of the Yang family defended the nation, many women in the family play an important role. The bravery and resourcefulness of such Yang family heroines as She Saihua, Yang Bajie (Sister Number Eight), Princess Chai and Mu Guiying exceeded that of male generals who struck terror into the hearts of the enemy. Even Yang Paifeng, a maidservant in the Yang household who was responsible for tending the hearth and serving tea, was also a warrior skilled in the martial arts.

The main purpose of this play is to give the protagonist Yang Paifeng a chance to display her skill in fighting. Although it recounts a tale of war and strife, the opera is full of humor and invariably delights its audiences.

-Ed.-

When Yang Paifeng returned after rendering meritorious service at the Three Passes, she resumed her old work of tending the fires in the great kitchen of the Tianbo Palace. In accordance with the orders issued by Yang Zongbao's grandmother, whoever rescued Yang Zongbao from the border region, where he had been captured by the Liao general Han Chang, and returned him to court would 'assume a high office and ride a magnificent steed'. Yang Paifeng deserved to have a grand title conferred upon her, but she rejected the

骑。"她是应该封官的。但她不愿意，情愿回到灶下来烧火，觉得还是干老本行自在。她从小就在太君房内干活，后来又分在大厨房里。整天价一根拨火棍不离手（自从她立下战功之后，这棍也长了身价，有了一个好名字，现在被人们称做"青龙棍"了），没事时摆弄，摸出了一套棍法。天波府里有男将也有女将，拿枪弄棒是平常事。看来看去，再笨的人也能看出一点门道来，何况她又聪明。可是没有谁知道她有这一身本领，连老太君也不知道，人们只知道她是个调皮的丫头。她也确是调皮。

排风从三关回来以后，身分不同了。尽管没有捞到什么官职，可是到底不同了。她走过时，男人都斜着眼看，露出一种异样的神色。倒不是嫉妒，她立了功可没有当官，没有什么可嫉妒的；可是觉得希奇，又不好意思向她打听。厨房里的小姊妹们就不同，一空下来就缠着她讲怎样打韩昌的。

"有什么可说的呢？还不是一棍两棍，打他的头，打他的腰膀，扫他的马腿，……韩昌就跑了。别看这些番邦上将人

honor in favor of returning to tend the kitchen fires in the belief that she would be more at ease with work she was familiar with. She was employed in the palace of the venerable Mrs. Yang since her childhood and worked in the kitchen, where the poker never left her hand throughout the day. After her glorious return, it was this poker that became famous as the Black Dragon Cudgel. In her idle moments she would play with the poker, creating new fighting techniques. Both male and female generals lived in the Tianbo Palace, and swordplay was as common an occurrence there as drinking tea. Merely by watching, even the most dim-witted person would be able to pick up some of their martial arts skills. Not a soul knew of Yang Paifeng's ability, not even Mrs. Yang. Most people thought of her as a mischievous young girl. How very right they were!

After returning from the Three Passes, Paifeng's status in the household changed. Although she hadn't beed granted an official post, when she walked by, men would glance at her with strange expressions. This wasn't jealousy, since with no official post she had nothing to arouse their envy, but all the same they felt she was a curiosity, and were even embarrassed to enquire about her. Her young sisters in the kitchen began to pester her for stories of her fight with Han Chang whenever the opportunity presented itself.

'What can I say? There was no exchange of blows; I merely struck him on the head, struck him on the waist, and swept his horse from under him. Then he ran away! Don't be taken in by overbearing generals who sit high in the saddle - they're all quite useless. So what is there to

高马大，气势汹汹，其实并不顶用。有什么可说的呢，跟平常在家里使家伙没有什么两样。不过瘾。"

排风两腿一翻，双手一摆，嘴角一撇，没话了。

小姊妹们听了也觉得无趣。

只有说起焦二爷焦赞，排风才忍不住想笑。人们也不懂她笑些什么。排风心里说，"难哪，出头难哪。打韩昌并不难，能上阵和韩昌交上手可真难哪！"

那一天孟二爷气急败坏地从边关赶回府里，见了太君报了军情，立即点将。太君说明了情由，立即下了赏号，好半日，黑压压满院子将校人等，没一个人吱声。"这可不是咱们天波府的规矩。"排风这时说起来还有气。"我是从人堆后面挤出来应声愿往。孟二爷一看笑了，开口就叫我'黄毛丫头'。见了太君，也不信我真有什么本事。你瞧，这可多难哪。三关之上，二十余员上将，个个都不是那韩昌的对手，我这'黄毛丫头'能成吗？

"点将是选拔人才。天波杨府能说没有人才吗？可是都让韩昌给镇住了。一个烧火的丫头能算人才吗？青龙棍烟薰火

tell? It was just like tending the fires at home. Nothing to get excited about.·

Paifeng sat there frowning and refused to say another word.

All the girls who were listening also found her story quite devoid of interest.

It was only when the name Jiao Zan was mentioned that Paifeng began to smile, though no one understood why. She thought to herself: ·It was so difficult getting involved in the first place. Beating Han Chang was easy, but going into battle and fighting him was really difficult.·

On that day, Meng Liang had returned flustered and desperate from the frontier passes to report the battle situation to Mrs. Yang, and suggested that officers be appointed. Mrs. Yang explained the situation to her men, stipulating the ranks and rewards to be given to successful warriors. For a long time, the officers filing the courtyard waited without a sound. ·This isn't the custom of the Tianbo Palace,· Paifeng remonstrated. ·It was I who squeezed my way out from behind the crowd of people, eager to fulfill the pressing task. When Meng Liang saw me, he laughed and called me a little girl. And when Mrs. Yang saw me, she also refused to believe I had any ability. You don't know how difficult it was. There were more than 20 leading generals there in the Three Passes, none of them a match for Han Chang. How could a ·little girl· hope to succeed?

·Generals are selected from the most talented soldiers. Since the Tianbo Palace generals were defeated by Han Chang, does this mean that there are no men of talent here? Can a slave girl who attends the fires be considered a person of

燎，刀枪架子上没有这一宗兵器。难怪孟二爷笑话，他给我的'鉴定'是，'上马无有拳头大，下马无有膝盖高。漫说是冲锋打仗，就是衬刀背、垫马蹄，也是不中用。'这话也不能说全无道理。这不能怪孟二爷，他光看表面上啦。孟二爷上了几岁年纪，胡子都一大把了。本事虽然不怎么样，人倒是挺忠厚的。他知错必改，花园比试，三下两下子就让我把他手里的家伙打脱了。接着他就趴在地上起不来了。他可真能服输，他领教了我的棍，服了，还在太君面前力保我去三关。这就是他的好处。大将到底有大将的风度。大将固然得凭手中的本事，可是还得凭肚量，凭一双能识人的眼睛。不能睁着眼睛在事实前面不认帐。自然，打赌打输了得给烧火的丫头赔礼，这在面子上一时下不来，是难怪的。瞧他那扭着头磨磨蹭蹭的样子……"排风扑哧一声笑了。

"唉，这是我闯过的头一关。

"孟二爷带着我到了三关，见了杨元帅。在这个地方我还有两关得闯，才能见得了韩昌的面。在三关上闯的后两关，和

talent? My Black Dragon Cudgel, stained by smoke and singed by fire, can hardly compare with the knives and spears stored in the armory, so it's not surprising that Meng Liang laughed. His appraisal of me was: 'On a horse she's no bigger than my fist; dismounted she barely comes up to my knees. As for going into battle, she could hardly withstand the dull edge of a sword or a horse's kick.' Meng Liang cannot be blamed for considering my appearance alone; he is getting on in years, and already has a long beard. Although he himself has little abililty, he is sincere and kindly nevertheless, and always corrects his errors when he becomes aware of them. When he was testing my fighting skills in the flower garden, I knocked his weapons out of his hands within seconds, and had him crawling on the ground. He is a man who knows how to acknowledge defeat. He endured my cudgel and admitted he was wrong; then in front of Mrs. Yang he did all he could to ensure I would go to the Three Passes - this is his good side. In the end, General Meng does have the demeanor of a great general. Of course, a great general has to rely on his own abilities; but he must also rely on his judgment to recongnize men of ability, and not refuse to admit mistakes in the face of facts. If he bets and loses, he must apologize, even to the little girl who tends the fires. This was understandably a very embarrassing loss of face for him. Just look how he turns away in shame ...' Yang Paifeng couldn't suppress a giggle.

Ah! This was the first pass I broke though.'

'Meng Liang led me to the Three Passes where I saw Commander Yang. But from there I still had to make my way through two more passes before meeting Han Chang face to

在天波府闯过的头关其实也没有什么两样。按理说，有了太君的将令和孟二爷的保单，元帅总该相信。可是不行，他们的眼光和孟二爷的一样，给我下的鉴定也是一样的。他们得试试，我到底有多少分量，他们得在手里掂一掂才算数。这就好嘛。眼见为实、耳听为虚嘛。

"元帅得有元帅的身分。他不能不遵太君的将令，可又将信将疑。这也难怪，他肩膀上的担子沉哪。可是杨元帅也够精明的，他支使焦二爷出面和我比武，他自己当保官。焦二爷赢了，他自然名正言顺地把我给太君退回去；输了，可又伤不了他的面子。

"提起焦赞焦二爷，那可真是。他也是三关上将。孟二爷是大红脸，焦二爷满脸锅底黑，就跟在大厨房的灶膛里刚扎了一头出去似的。他可没有孟王爷那么忠厚老实，多着一个心眼。可是说来说去，他到底还是个大好人。忠心耿耿，就是办事毛手毛脚。小本官去给老元戎上坟插柳，就是他放了一炮，惊动了韩昌，才被辽兵擒去的。

face. The last two passes I stormed were really no different from the first pass I had broken through at the Tianbo Palace. Normally, with Mrs. Yang's orders and Meng Liang's guarantee, Commander Yang should have believed in me, but he failed to. He assessed me in the same manner as Meng Liang. They had to test me, to weigh me in the palms of their own hands: You can believe your eyes, but not necessarily believe your ears.

'A supreme commander must have the dignity of a supreme commander. He may not disobey his mother's orders, but now he half-believes and half-doubts. This is pardonable, for the weight of responsibility that lies on his shoulders is indeed heavy. But Commander Yang is wily; he supported Jiao Zan when testing me in competition, and himself stood as guarantor. Should Jiao Zan win, he would be justified in sending me back to Mrs. Yang. But, if he lost, it would do no damage to his own reputation.

'Jiao Zan really is the limit! He, too, is one of the star generals of the Three Passes. Meng Liang had a great red face, but Jiao Zan's was as black as the bottom of a cooking pot. He looks like he has just pulled his head out of the kichen stove. He is less honest and tolerant than Meng Liang, though he is thoughtful and circumspect. When all is said and done, he's still a good man, faithful and true. It's just that he's rather careless in handing his affairs. When Yang Zongbao visited the grave of his grandfather, the old supreme commander, to plant a willow, it was Jiao Zan who set off a firecracker and aroused Han Chang, whereupon the Liao soldiers captured him.

"焦二爷劈头就问他的孟二哥,'兵搬多少,大将几员?'他万没有料到,搬来的就是我这么一个烧火的小丫头。一见他,我就禁不住想笑。活像一名头号的火头军。果不然,焦二爷朝我一打量,也笑了。怪就怪在他说的那些话跟孟二爷在天波府里说的竟是一模一样。

"孟二爷不但撺掇着焦二爷跟我比试,打了赌,还拖杨元帅当了保官,还嘱咐我到了校场,尽管拿出本事来,用不着担心。万一失了手有他承当。这当口,不用说焦赞,就是杨元帅也满肚子狐疑,拿不准,只有孟良心里有数。要说他成心使坏,给焦赞当上,那倒也不是。想凭两句话就说服焦赞可没那么容易,最方便、最直截了当的办法莫如让他亲身领教一下。他们三位是结拜兄弟,彼此的脾气摸得清楚。孟二爷明白,他自己走过的路,非得让焦二爷也照样走一遍不可。靠空口白舌,不行。

"没有交手之前,是我先给焦二爷施了一礼,我说,'我怕失手打着二爷,莫要见怪!'他一听,就喳喳喳地叫了起来,他气急了。一交手我又假意败下阵去,把焦二爷引到无人之处。这也是为了给他留点面子,免得大庭广众之中丢人现眼。等杨元帅带着孟二爷赶到时,焦二爷早就趴在地上,站不起来了。"

'Right at the start, Jiao Zan asked Meng Liang: 'How many soldiers are being transferred here and how many generals?' He never imagined that it was only me, a girl who tended the fires. When I saw him, I couldn't help but laugh. He was the spitting image of a first rate army cook. Unexpectedly, Jiao Zan sized me up and began to laugh as well. What is strange is that his words were identical to those of Meng Liang at the Tianbo Palace.

'Meng Liang not only urged Jiao Zan to compete with me, but also made a bet and entrusted Commander Yang to act as guarantor. He enjoined me to use all of my skills in the arena and told me that he would take responsibility for any accidents. At this time there is no need to mention that Jiao Zan and Commander Yang were both very suspicious. Only Meng Liang was sure of what he was doing. But to say that he was deliberately playing a dirty trick in order to fool Jiao Zan is not true either. Jiao Zan is stubborn. The best way to convince him is to allow him to learn for himself. The three of them are sworn brothers, well aware of each other's temperament. Meng Liang knows that Jiao Zan must be made to traverse the path that he himself has already taken. Mere words will not suffice.

'Before we engaged in conflict, I first saluted Jiao Zan: 'General Jiao, should I strike you by a slip of the hand, pray do not blame me.' Hearing this he became flustered and began to stutter. I pretended to be losing and let him preserve a little of his self-respect. By the time Commander Yang led Meng Liang to the arena, Jiao Zan had long since been crawling on the ground, unable to get up.'

　　排风这小妮子，走出天波府，来到三关，打败了韩昌，救回了杨宗保，经了风雨，见了世面。在她自己，也不过就像赶了一趟庙会一样。打韩昌，其实倒并没有花费多大气力。倒是一个烧火的丫头想披挂上阵可真不容易。她连闯三关，不只用棍，还施展了一个女孩子的聪明、爱娇……才得如愿。她总是忘不了那些好人，孟二爷、焦二爷、杨元帅……她一想起自己用了什么方法才说服了这些好人，放她上阵把韩昌打倒，就觉得非常有意思。她在回忆，述说这前后的一切时，脸上总是漾着笑。就像好不容易到底赶了一次庙会似的。

Yang Paifeng left the Tianbo Palace and arrived at the Three Passes where she defeated Han Chang and rescued Yang Zongbao. To her, this difficult venture was as easy as taking a trip to the temple fair. In fact, it required very little effort for her to beat Han Chang. But for a girl who tends the fires to even think of strapping on armor and entering into battle is no mean achievement. She broke through the three passes by using her cudgel as well as her intelligence and charm. She never forgot those good men, Meng Liang, Jiao Zan and Commander Yang ... She smiled when she thought of what she had to go through to convince these good men to let her go into battle. It was as if she had to surmount a thousand difficulties in order to attend a temple fair.

This book is edited and designed by the Editorial Committee of *Cultural China* series

Managing Directors: Wang Youbu, Xu Naiqing
Editorial Director: Wu Ying
Editors: Wu Ying, Yang Xinci

Chinese Text by Huang Shang
Translation provided by New World Press

Interior and Cover Design: Yuan Yinchang, Hu Bin

ISBN-13: 978-1-60220-912-1

Address any comments about *Shower of Flowers: Tales from Beijing Opera (1)* to:

Better Link Press
99 Park Ave
New York, NY 10016
USA
or
Shanghai Press and Publishing Development Company
F 7 Donghu Road, Shanghai, China (200031)
Email: comments_betterlinkpress@hotmail.com

Computer typeset by Yuan Yinchang Design Studio, Shanghai
Printed in China by Shanghai Donnelley Printing Co. Ltd.

1 2 3 4 5 6 7 8 9 10